Ballet  *Academy*

Find out more about the characters
and the Academy at:

www.balletacademy.co.uk

The *Ballet Academy* series

1) Dance Steps
2) A Question of Character
3) Friends Old and New
4) On Your Toes
5) Dancing In Milan
6) A Tutu Too Many

Companion book:
The World of Ballet

Dancing in Milan

BEATRICE MASINI

Translation by Laura Watkinson

PICCADILLY PRESS · LONDON

First published in Great Britain in 2010
by Piccadilly Press Ltd,
5 Castle Road, London NW1 8PR
www.piccadillypress.co.uk

Text copyright © Beatrice Masini, 2006
English language translation © Laura Watkinson 2009
Translated from the original *La Scuola di Londra*,
published by Edizioni EL, Trieste, Italy
www.edizioniel.com
Published by arrangement with Rights People, London

A catalogue record for this book is available
from the British Library

ISBN: 978 1 84812 078 5

Printed in the UK by CPI Bookmarque, Croydon, CR0 4TD
Cover design by Patrick Knowles
Cover illustration by Sara Not

Mixed Sources
Product group from well-managed
forests and other controlled sources
www.fsc.org Cert no. TT-COC-002227
© 1996 Forest Stewardship Council
FSC

CHAPTER ONE

News
and Surprises

Zoe had often thought that, when it came to dance, one person's misfortune could turn out to be someone else's good luck. So when her best friend told her the news, she wasn't entirely surprised.

'Have you heard?' Leda had exclaimed, barely able to contain herself. 'There are three spare places on the summer course in Milan!'

'How did that happen?' Zoe asked. 'I thought the whole of Year Ten were going.'

'They were, but one of them dropped out and two of them failed their exams. Isn't that great?' she'd replied.

The history of ballet is full of stories about stars who were discovered almost by chance. They'd often been the understudy for a prima ballerina who had suddenly fallen ill or twisted her ankle at the dress rehearsal. You were out and someone else was in. It was harsh, but that's just the way it was.

Zoe didn't quite share Leda's enthusiasm about the unexpected opportunity. Zoe gave her a thoughtful, slightly distant look. There might be three places available, she reasoned, but there were twenty-five students in their year alone, so the chances of being picked were slim, especially with other older, more experienced students to consider too. Anyway, she thought to herself, she wasn't even sure she wanted to go to Milan. A whole fortnight in a big foreign city that you didn't know, being bossed around and assessed by teachers who you didn't know either, but who were bound to be scary. It wasn't Zoe's idea of a fun summer.

Then she smiled to herself. She knew it was a case of sour grapes, thinking that if she couldn't have it, she might as well decide she didn't want it anyway, and that it wouldn't have been the right thing for her in the first place.

Leda, however, just rattled away about what she'd do if she went to Milan, without paying any attention to the range of expressions passing over her friend's face – vague enthusiasm, bewilderment, then indifference, quiet resignation, and finally relief. 'And you know the school's right in the centre of town and the place is absolutely packed with all these wonderful designer shops. You can pick up unique things that you just don't see in the shops here . . .'

It was typical of Leda to turn everything into an opportunity for a shopping spree. Or at least, it was typical of the way Leda was lately.

'I'm not interested in going round and looking at any of those old churches or paintings,' Leda continued. 'I saw them when I went with my mum. I wouldn't mind going up on the roof of the cathedral again though. The view from the top of the Duomo – that's what they call the cathedral – is absolutely incredible. You can see the mountains in the distance. Oh, and you can see right into the top floor of this fantastic department store from there too. There's a café up there and they do the most —'

'Leda, Leda!' cried Zoe. 'Earth to Leda! Come in, Leda!'

'Ha ha. What do you want?'

'You know, Madame might decide not to fill those empty spaces. That's what happened last year. Remember?'

'Oh, but this year it's different. Trust me. I have my sources. Alissa heard Madame talking to the secretary and she said they'd need to decide within two days who was going so that they could get all the paperwork done in time. Can you imagine? Two whole weeks with the Year Tens! So you'll probably get to meet loads of older boys too. But, of course, you've got Alex, so you probably think fourteen-year-olds are just little babies.'

'You know, you are such an idiot sometimes,' Zoe blurted out. Alex was an older student who had chatted to Zoe a few times, but that was all. Unfortunately, the gossip round the school, spread mainly by Leda, had suggested there was something between them, which simply wasn't the case.

Leda paused for a moment. Zoe welcomed the silence. 'Sorry,' Leda continued, and for the first time in ten minutes she appeared to be focusing on something that was not the remote possibility of a summer course in Milan. 'I should just keep my mouth closed and put a lid on my imagination. That way I'd avoid a whole lot of trouble.'

Exactly, thought Zoe. All of the gossip and misunder-standings about Zoe and Alex had threatened to ruin her relationship with Roberto only a couple of months before. Things had been very uncomfortable between her and Roberto for a while, as though they were scared of offend-ing or hurting each other. Fortunately, things improved and had returned almost to the way they were before, but there was still an awkwardness, a slight hesitation between them, as though the two of them had to get used to each other all over again. *But maybe it was nothing to do with Alex*, Zoe pondered. *Maybe it would have happened anyway.*

There was another long silence. That silence contained a lot of things: an exchange of glances – one embarrassed and the other slightly annoyed, fleeting thoughts, assumptions . . . Then Zoe reached out a hand and gave Leda's shoulder a squeeze, and everything went back to normal.

That was the nice thing about good friends, thought Zoe. She knew Leda hadn't really meant anything by her comment, just as Leda understood why Zoe had snapped at her. It was easy to forgive each other.

They were in the playground, beneath the magnolia, enjoying the cool shade. The school term and exams had finished, but they still popped into the Academy sometimes, partly out of habit and partly because everyone did. They were all allowed to use the practice rooms throughout the holidays, and there was nearly always someone else there you could have a chat with, so it still felt like everyone was really part of something special. It was as though the Academy called out to them, irresistibly, when they weren't forced to go in every day. The atmosphere was so calm and relaxed, but for some reason they all seemed to stick to the usual rules of silence, order and discipline.

The Academy was such a fascinating, intriguing place. That was one of the reasons Zoe loved it. Thinking about it, she couldn't come up with a single thing that she didn't like about her school – unlike Leda, who was already launching into a monologue that Zoe had heard many times before.

'I'm bored. I am sooo fed up. It's always the same old things. Always the same old faces. This summer course in Milan would be great for us. It's time we went out and explored the world a bit.'

'You could always decide to be an explorer when you grow up. Or maybe a tour guide, which wouldn't be quite so dangerous . . .'

Leda rolled her eyes. 'Laugh at me all you like. Don't you want to grow up, and do whatever you feel like doing? There's so much exciting stuff out there . . .'

That had been one of Leda's favourite topics recently. She was so fidgety and restless. Zoe didn't feel that way at all. Of course, she wanted to grow up too, but she wanted to do it in her own good time, so that she didn't miss out on anything along the way. She thought she'd probably grow up to be a professional ballet dancer, but she didn't know that for sure. Why was there such a rush to decide for certain?

'I don't see it the same way as you,' Zoe replied. 'I think our lives are pretty exciting as they are. Think of all the nerves and excitement we have before recitals and exams, and waiting for the results to come out – all that suspense.'

'I know. But that's because you know how to make the best of things. I actually envy you, Zoe. You know how to appreciate the little things in life. I always . . . want more. Perhaps it's because I'm an only child. What do you think?'

'Maybe,' Zoe said, her eyes twinkling. 'You're certainly very demanding.'

'And I always get whatever I want,' Leda said with a smile. Then her smile vanished and she added, 'Well, nearly always.'

Zoe knew exactly what her friend was talking about. Leda had recently decided that Lucas, one of their best friends, was the perfect boy for her and she'd set out to conquer him like a general leading an army. She hadn't succeeded though. Lucas had let her drag him along on dates for a while, but then he'd backed off. Zoe had thought he was simply biding his time, but in the end he said that he really wasn't interested in having a relationship like that, and didn't want to lead Leda on. He just wasn't convinced he saw Leda as more than a friend, and as soon as he'd realised how he felt, he'd put a stop to the dating.

Zoe couldn't say that she was really sad or upset about Leda and Lucas. In fact, she actually envied them slightly and wondered if things would be easier and nicer if she were just friends with Roberto. Everything worked out really well when it was all about friendship. Zoe was glad that the incident with Leda hadn't spoiled her friendship with Lucas, which went back to their first year at school and their very first dance lessons. In fact, she and Lucas were always phoning each other, meeting up, and things were exactly how they had always been.

Her friendship with Leda had got stronger again since the two of them had started spending more time alone together. It felt like it had when they were younger, and boys were just something to giggle and daydream about. It was all part of growing up: bravely facing changes, and not being silly and missing what you had a short while ago. What was just around the corner was mysterious, but very exciting. As Leda said, Zoe knew how to appreciate the little things in life – she always looked for the positive aspects of every situation, the silver lining of every cloud.

Ha, I'm so wise and insightful, Zoe thought to herself with a grin. Sometimes she thought she'd like to be a bit more scatterbrained, like Leda. But she knew that she couldn't just change her personality. Anyway, there was already one airhead in the friendship and two would be absolute chaos. Maybe things were really fine as they were.

'Just imagine how boring summer's going to be otherwise,' Leda was carrying on. 'Going to the seaside with Mum, then on holiday with Dad. Same old places, same old faces. I feel like I'm going backwards, not forwards in life. Don't be surprised if I'm a year younger when school starts again, and I turn up with plaits in my hair like Pippi Longstocking.'

Zoe just smiled and shook her head. 'You never know,

maybe this time you'll meet some new people. Boys, even.'

'Yeah, right. The beach will be packed with little kids and old grannies, as usual. And you're lucky if you see a rabbit at Dad's place in the countryside, let alone a person. If you do happen to see someone, it's big news and you have to run and tell everybody. When I say everybody, I mean all of the trees. At least you're going to be having fun with Alice in the mountains. I am so, so jealous.'

'No, you're not. If you were really jealous, you wouldn't tell me,' Zoe pointed out. 'You'd just stand there pulling a sulky face and not saying anything. Whereas, in actual fact, you've been rattling away like a runaway train!'

'You're right. I'm not jealous of Alice. I actually think she's quite nice. Although, I have to say . . .' Leda managed to stop herself, but opened her eyes wide, as though she was boggling at something in surprise.

Zoe laughed. 'I know, you don't think much of her dress sense.'

'Sense? There's nothing sensible about it. The girl quite simply has no idea how to dress,' Leda stated firmly. 'Mind you, I'm sure they don't have any of our decent city shops in that little town she comes from. What a nightmare. Anyway, what did you say her brothers were like? Cute?'

Zoe smiled, and she was about to start describing them, when they heard someone shouting their names.

'Leda! Zoe!'

They turned round at the same time and were both completely amazed to see that it was Laila calling them, from the top of the playground steps. Her face was completely red, which was a very odd sight. She was usually the perfect little ballerina, composed and dignified from head to toe. She came down the stairs and walked towards them with the distinctive walk of someone who started dancing when they were very young. She was smiling. Smiling?!

She's got something nasty to tell us, Zoe suspected. Then she felt ashamed for having thought that. But it was Laila after all, and almost everything she said was mean.

'I'm going to Milan!' Laila announced, as soon as she reached them. She looked really excited. 'They've chosen me to go to Milan. Isn't that wonderful?'

'Fantastic,' said Leda sarcastically, her mouth twisted in a sneer that she didn't even try to hide.

'Well done,' Zoe said, simply.

Zoe didn't like Laila much. In fact, there had been moments in the past when she hadn't liked her at all, but there was no denying that she was a good dancer. Zoe had no idea what else to say, though. They'd been in the same class since they started school, but there wasn't even the slightest spark of friendship between them. In fact, Laila didn't have *any* real friends. She was cut off, closed away in her bubble of perfection. Whenever she stepped out of it, it was only to make cutting remarks to the others, her perfection crumbling and giving way to spitefulness. Zoe sometimes suspected that Laila was much more fragile than she wanted people to think and that her meanness was just an extreme form of self-defence, but it was hard to be friendly towards someone who put you down all the time, and there was no excuse for being as nasty as she tended to be.

Whatever the case, it was obvious that the three girls didn't have much to say to each other as they stood there in the shade of the magnolia. Laila finally broke the silence. 'I don't know who the other two are. It could be one of you. Who knows?'

'When are you going?' Zoe asked her.

'In two weeks. I was supposed to be staying with my grandma in France, but this is so much better.'

'Such a pity you can't speak Italian as well as French, eh?' Leda said nastily.

In actual fact, even though Laila was so good at all her ballet lessons, she wasn't quite as gifted at proper school subjects. She always managed to get by, somehow or other, but her school report was far from enviable. Except, of course, for French. Her dad was French, so she could speak and write it fluently.

'You know, it's quite similar to French. I may be able to learn some Italian while I'm there,' Laila replied. 'Then again, I won't really have much time. The course is very intensive. I spoke to one of the girls who went last year.'

Zoe could have been mistaken, but she thought she saw a cloud of worry pass across Laila's perfect doll-like face. Was it possible that she was already feeling a little nervous about the hard work to come? That wasn't like Laila.

'I'd really like it if they picked one of you,' Laila said suddenly.

Leda stared at Laila with her mouth open. She looked so much like an amazed cartoon character that Zoe almost burst out laughing, but just managed to stop herself. She didn't know how Laila would react. She could be so touchy. Still, Zoe had to ask, 'Why's that?'

'Oh, I don't know,' Laila answered in her slight French accent. 'A new place, new teachers . . . I'd like to be with someone I know.'

Well, that makes no sense, Zoe's inner voice replied, *because you don't really know us either.* She didn't say it out loud though. Why would she want to? All she'd do was offend a classmate who didn't even really matter to her.

Leda couldn't help herself though. 'At least you'll get the chance to go shopping for some decent clothes while you're there,' she said, looking Laila up and down with a calculating and superior expression.

That wasn't a nice thing to say, even if Laila deserves it, Zoe thought. Laila might have been the model ballet student, but she wore the strangest clothes: little ankle socks that a four-year-old would wear, baby shoes with straps and buckles . . . All she needed was a nice little rounded collar and she'd have looked just right for nursery school.

But Laila didn't care anyway. She shrugged her shoulders and gave a little smile. '*Maman* thinks I look fine like this . . . and clothes aren't important. What counts is talent. See you later.' And Laila walked away, with her perfect ballerina posture, head always held slightly higher than necessary, as though the world were a huge stage to perform upon.

'Can you imagine what a pain that would be, ending up in Milan with her?' Leda grumbled. 'You know what? I've completely gone off the idea. My holiday plans are sounding pretty good right now.'

'You didn't need to give her such a hard time about her clothes,' Zoe said quietly, shaking her head. 'Laila's right really. The shoes you wear are less important than talent – and that's something you can't buy.'

'Oh, I hate it when you get all serious,' said Leda. 'Why can't you be silly sometimes, just to make me happy?'

The two girls looked at each other and burst out laughing.

CHAPTER TWO

The Big Announcement

There was a strange atmosphere around the dinner table that evening. No one said anything, but Maria and Sara kept looking at their sister and exchanging meaningful glances, as if they knew something that Zoe didn't. Finally, Maria broke the silence. 'Mum, Mum, when are you going to tell her?'

'Calm down, Maria, let's finish our dinner first,' Dad said. 'Sara, how could you possibly leave my delicious pie half-eaten?'

Sara smiled apologetically and pushed away her plate. 'I'm not very hungry this evening.'

'You haven't been very hungry for a while,' their mum commented. 'You haven't suddenly decided to go on a diet, have you? Because you really don't need to.'

'I know,' Sara said with a sigh. 'That's not what it is, Mum. Honestly, I'm just not very hungry.'

Zoe didn't pay too much attention to what they were saying; she couldn't really concentrate on the crisp, golden crust of the pie or her big sister's worries because she was so curious about this piece of news that she was going to find out about. She had a suspicion what it might be – something about Sara having some problems at school. She'd always been brilliant, but Zoe hadn't seen her with her schoolbooks recently, which was strange because it was exam time.

But the secret turned out to be something completely different. By the time pudding arrived, Maria just couldn't keep it in any longer. 'Can I tell her now? Please?'

Mum nodded.

Maria turned to Zoe and shouted, 'They've chosen you for the summer course in Milan! You're leaving in two weeks! Are you happy? You're happy, aren't you?'

Zoe was silent, as she had been for most of the meal. Then she whispered just three words. 'Are you sure?'

'Absolutely,' her dad said, looking up from his pudding. 'Madame Olenska herself made the phone call. She spoke to Maria.'

'Oh, I wonder if Maria made a mistake,' Zoe blurted out. Then, seeing her little sister's crestfallen face, she added, 'Oh, no, Maria, I didn't mean . . . I just thought maybe someone was having a joke.'

'Don't worry. Maria asked Madame Olenska what she was calling about, then passed the phone to me. It's all true,' her mum said.

'Okay,' Zoe replied. That was all she could manage to get out. After they'd chosen Laila, it seemed such a remote possibility that they'd ever choose Zoe that she'd not even really thought about it, and she hadn't been particularly bothered. Until now.

'Why me?' she couldn't help but wonder out loud, after a long moment of silence when she could feel everyone else staring at her.

'Why not?' her dad asked. 'Don't you think you're good enough?' He smiled at her. 'If that's the case, you're obviously wrong.'

Is that what I think? That I'm not good enough? Zoe wondered later, when she was lying in bed.

Am I scared of being compared with other dancers? Do I think I'm not going to be up to the challenge? That Laila and the older students will all be so much better at following the instructions of some brilliant Italian teacher who's seen all the best dancers in the world?

All those muddled questions ran through her head and she couldn't get to sleep. Insomnia felt like a very grown-up thing to have, but it was a grown-up thing she'd have been happy to do without. Falling asleep, feeling calm, happy, contented, was so much better. Staying awake because your adrenalin levels had rocketed and you were so excited was fun, like on a sleepover, but Zoe suspected it was something else that was keeping her eyes wide open and fixed on the ceiling. A sort of . . . yes, that's what it was . . . a sort of fear. She hadn't even told Leda, or Lucas, or Roberto yet, even though a quick text message would have done it. She could hardly even bring herself to say it out loud.

Her mum must have sensed that something was up. Zoe's clock said it was 11:11, and her mum was usually curled up in bed with a book by that time, but Zoe saw her silhouetted in her bedroom doorway, peering around the half-open door.

'Oh, hi, Mum,' she whispered. 'I can't get to sleep.'

'I thought as much,' her mum answered. She slipped through the door and came over to sit beside Zoe on the bed. In the dim light from the street outside, Zoe could see her mum was wearing her nice dark blue pyjamas, which looked both masculine and pretty at the same time. Zoe reached out to stroke the sleeve. The silk felt strange beneath her fingers – so soft and smooth.

'Are you worrying about things?' she whispered.

'I don't know,' Zoe replied, and that was the truth. 'I think it's amazing . . . and wonderful. But I don't know whether I really want to go. It's not like I can say no, though, is it?'

'I don't think so,' her mum agreed. 'Madame Olenska would be very disappointed with you. Anyway, I think it would do you some good to get away for a while, from us, from the normal things you do. It's good to face challenges.'

'Yes, well, a lot of nasty medicines do you good,' Zoe said, 'but no one ever wants to take them.'

Her mum laughed quietly. 'There are some things that you have to do, just to try them out and see if they're the right thing for you. It's certainly a bit early on in your career, but at least it'll give you a taste of what life's like for a real ballerina. All the touring, living out of a suitcase, the loneliness, new places to see and new ways of doing things . . . You'll have to pick everything up so quickly.'

'What if I don't like it?'

'Then it's better to find out now than in five years' time. You can always change your mind, change your life even. You know what your dad and I think about it. Nothing's decided, nothing's fixed. If it's what you want to do, do it. But only if you're really sure. A ballerina's life is so intense. You can't go into it half-heartedly.'

'Isn't it strange?' Zoe said after a while. 'It all seems

so simple on stage, so natural. You don't think about everything that goes into being a ballet dancer. Years of study and hard work, then the challenge of going far away from home and staying away for long stretches at a time.'

'That's right,' her mum said. 'That's why I think it's better to find out as soon as possible whether it's right for you. This summer course could help you to decide. There's no pressure; the chance just fell into your lap. And that's exactly why I think you need to seize the opportunity. And . . . I also have a list of very nice shops you might like to visit . . .'

Zoe's mum kissed her goodnight, and Zoe soon fell asleep with a mental image of herself, her mum and Sara (Maria was off somewhere else, probably in some beautiful park, chasing squirrels with Dad) loaded with shopping bags, like those actresses in television shows, laughing and walking along and bumping into one another and laughing again; three happy friends with the world at their feet. The thought was enough, at least for the moment, to cancel out that other mental image, still hazy and vague, of herself dragging a suitcase along in an unfamiliar country, not knowing whether to go out and conquer the world or to just give up, sit down on her suitcase and get someone to come and fetch her, someone who could look after her.

* * *

Zoe and Leda went to their favourite café in the park the next day. They sat there with two dishes of ice cream that were slowly melting away. Leda had been holding her spoon in the air for a good ten minutes, as though she had turned to stone. Her mouth certainly wasn't still though. She was asking so many questions that Zoe had stopped eating her ice cream too, just so she could answer.

Before meeting Leda, she'd gone round to the school to find out all about the course and to pick up the information sheets with lists of clothes and everything she needed to take with her to Milan. She was pretty well informed – and so was Leda now. Leda eventually fell silent, and was looking down at the melted mess of chocolate and strawberry ice cream in the metal dish. Then she mixed together the swirls of pink and brown and sighed. 'Wouldn't it have been nice if they'd chosen me instead of Laila?' she said. 'We could have gone together and shared a room.'

'It says here that the rooms are single,' Zoe said, leafing through the sheets of paper that the scary school secretary had handed to her with an expression that could almost have passed for a smile.

'Phew, at least you won't have the torture of sharing with Laila, then. You're going to have her clinging to you the rest of the time anyway.'

'Oh, but she's not the only one going. They've chosen

Charlotte from the year above too. And then there are all the Year Tens who are going anyway.'

'I'm so envious. You're going to come back with all these new friends. Next year you won't even want to look at us little ones,' Leda said.

'You? A little one?' Zoe grinned at her tall friend. 'Hardly!'

'Oh, what a disaster! What an absolute disaster!' Leda continued, as though she hadn't heard a word. 'The group's breaking up. Lucas runs away whenever he sees me coming and you're scaring Roberto away.'

'Very funny! You know he's just going to stay with his grandparents in Italy, like he does every year.'

'Yes, I know, but you've hardly been spending any time together, have you? And now with this trip to Milan . . .'

'What's Milan got to do with it?' Zoe said, with a touch of irritation.

'Oh, Milan's got everything to do with it. I know what you're up to. You're going to use the opportunity to make a fresh start, and look for new opportunities. After all, what am I? I'm just boring old Leda. I wouldn't blame you for being tired of me.'

'I've never thought anything of the sort,' Zoe told her. 'But you're pretty boring when you go on like that. Anyway, I'm only going away for a fortnight, not for six months! I'll be back at the beginning of August. We'll be able to see each other before you go away with your mum and I'll tell you all about it. Do you really think that I can have a complete life make-over in two weeks?'

Leda didn't say anything. She picked up the metal dish, drank the contents, banged the dish back down on the table and looked at Zoe. 'You're right,' she said. 'I was exaggerating. But, given the importance of the occasion, I thought a little drama would be appropriate.

'It's an amazing opportunity – I can see that, even if I'm not that interested in classical dance. Where you're going in Milan it's all pointes and tutus. No, America's where I want to go. Maybe next year. It seems more . . . suitable for my crazy personality. New York, don't you think?'

Zoe laughed. Leda was really crazy, sometimes. Completely unhinged. She was sure of one thing though: Leda really wasn't envious of her. Zoe knew that Leda was too kind to be jealous of her good luck. And indeed, Leda finally declared, 'I'm so, so happy for you, Zoe. But you have to promise me you'll bring me back a beautiful top from one of those gorgeous shops in Milan.'

'What colour? Fuchsia?' Zoe asked.

'Of course. But now that I think about it, I quite like purple too, as long as it's not proper dark purple, more a kind of violet, you know?'

'You are so impossible,' said Zoe, smiling.

'I know. But that's why you love me.'

Zoe had to admit it was true, and showed it with a hug.

CHAPTER THREE

Flying into the Future

'How do I do it up? Like this?'

Zoe was used to having a little sister, so she found it surprisingly easy to be patient with Laila. She leaned over Laila, who was sitting beside her, and fastened her seatbelt. Click. Done. Then she looked out of the window at the dry grass alongside the runway.

It was a misty morning, but you could tell it was going to be a nice day. The group had spent two hours hanging around the airport, suspended somewhere between home and abroad. Mums and dads had said their farewells, waving their last goodbyes as their teacher Gimenez had led what she called the 'gang' through passport control and security checks. Zoe had sent her dad away as soon as she saw Gimenez, dressed in her trademark red and black, as unmistakable as ever. A hug and he was gone. Laila's mum had stayed longer, fussing over Laila, before finally saying goodbye. Then Laila, putting aside any of her last remnants of pride, had glued herself to Zoe the moment she saw her and she didn't show any sign of wanting to leave her side.

'This is the first time I've ever flown, you know,' she revealed to Zoe, slightly embarrassed, so Zoe had to take on the role of an experienced travelling companion. At least now that they were about to take off, Laila might calm down a little. It wasn't really the poor girl's fault; she was just a bit nervous. If Leda had been there, she'd have taken the opportunity to get her own back for all of the rudeness, the sarcastic comments and the gossip that she'd had to suffer in the years she'd been forced to spend with Laila. Zoe could imagine Leda's thoughts: *Ha, it's time for you to pay, my dear Laila, and it's going to be expensive.*

Although Zoe had also had some memorable clashes with Laila when they were younger (and not all that long ago either, to tell the truth), she decided to let it go. She was actually quite surprised at her own generosity, but she also thought it would be nice to have a familiar face close by, and didn't want to push her away. They were in this together.

She wasn't sure she wanted the familiar face to be quite as close as it was, though. Laila made sure she was only a few centimetres away at any time. They had gone to have a quick look around the duty free shop together and bought various different types of sweets (necessary provisions for two girls on a journey), and they'd gone to the loo together. Zoe had waited patiently while Laila touched up her kiwi-flavour lip-gloss, and studied her face in the harsh fluorescent light.

My face is thinner than usual, Zoe had thought to herself. *Sara's not eating, but I'm losing weight. Is that good or bad?* But she didn't answer her own question.

Now her neighbour on the plane, who seemed calmer once she'd passed the flight attendant's seatbelt inspection, was happily unwrapping her fruit sweets. Zoe chose a mandarin-flavoured one and let the sugar melt on to her tongue as the plane raced down the runway, and then it was up, up and away. She could feel a line of fingertips digging into her forearm, but the grip soon loosened.

'We're on our way,' she said to Laila. 'We're flying.' There was a nicer view through the window now, as the ground below became smaller and smaller and everything scaled down to the size of a model, until it looked more like a map than a real place. They kept climbing upwards and soon all Zoe could see was sky, a shifting, changing landscape of blue and white.

Laila was fidgeting and Zoe could tell that she wanted to talk to her now she was over the first wave of panic, but she didn't really know her all that well and she didn't have much to say to her. It all felt a bit strange to Zoe, so she just took out her book, casting a few sidelong glances to check on Laila but trying not to attract her attention or give her any excuse for conversation. She wanted to spend time in silence just sitting there calmly, reading a bit and thinking.

Roberto had phoned her the day before and he'd promised to come and meet her in Milan, towards the end of the course, when he would be staying nearby with his grandparents. He'd been really nice and wished her good luck and said he was happy for her. He sounded genuinely pleased and Zoe realised that she did miss him. She thought that maybe it was time to stop being annoyed with him about the jealous way he'd reacted to the gossip about Alex. They'd gone out for a pizza together the evening before he'd left, with both of their families, and it had been so much fun, so easy and normal – two real friends saying goodbye for a little while.

But now she was doing something by herself – no family, no friends around her. Madame Olenska hadn't given her any deep and meaningful advice when Zoe popped into school to thank her before leaving. All she said was, 'I hope that it will be a wonderful experience for you,' and she shook her hand the way grown-ups do. As Zoe left Madame's office, she'd realised that she did in fact feel a bit older now, stepping out on her own. The feeling had quickly faded that morning when Gimenez had warned all of them, 'Do not leave the group. If you get lost, call me immediately on my mobile.' Gimenez was, of course, solely responsible for the safety of twelve pupils, so it was only natural that she'd behave a bit like a mother hen, even though she wasn't normally like that.

Then, just before she'd turned her phone off as instructed, a message from Leda had arrived. Zoe had realised Leda must have set her alarm clock so that she could send the text at eight in the morning. It was the summer holidays, after all. *U STAR!!! ALL GROWN UP NOW!!! GD LUCK Z!!! XXX*, she'd written, all in capital letters.

Zoe felt as though the world was sending her mixed messages: some people treated her as though she'd suddenly grown up, but with others it was like she was still just a little girl. She knew for certain that, as far as her mum was concerned, she was simply Zoe – no more, no less. All her mum had done when she'd said goodbye was give her a big hug and whisper 'I love you' in her ear, which was exactly what Zoe had needed to hear.

She sighed to herself. *Well, I really am on my own now.* When the stewardess came round with the breakfast,

Zoe realised that she had fallen asleep, and awoke to see that Laila was starting to panic again. She really did feel pretty grown up as she pulled Laila's tray down for her as though she was her mum, and asked for an orange juice for her.

'Thank you,' Laila whispered, which, coming from her, was worth a lot, because she was usually the type who acted as though the world owed her something, but now they were up there in the sky, the rules of the world had been left behind.

Charlotte from the year above was sitting in the seat behind them with one of the Year Tens, a girl who'd been her friend since they were little. They were chatting and laughing away. Zoe wondered how she'd have felt if Leda, or Lucas, had been sitting beside her, instead of Laila. But perhaps she didn't actually want either of them to be there, because the time had definitely come for her to do something on her own. Laila obviously didn't count as company. She was just someone she knew, not a real friend.

Gimenez walked down the aisle, an unlikely stewardess and also an unlikely 'gang' leader. You could see she was feeling more relaxed now: a coach would be waiting for them at the airport, which would take them to the hotel where they were staying, so they wouldn't even need to work out how to get there on the unfamiliar public-transport system.

'Had your breakfast, girls? The jam tart was actually quite tasty.'

Zoe nodded and smiled. How did Gimenez manage to keep her lipstick perfectly in place even after eating? It was a mystery. Maybe she'd had her lips tattooed, as Leda had once suggested. She said you could have your eyebrows tattooed or permanent eyeliner, so why shouldn't you be able to get your lips tattooed too? Laila, on the other hand, had managed to lick off all of her lip-gloss, along with the crumbs, and she was reapplying it very carefully, looking at herself in a tiny mirror. The scent of kiwi filled the air.

'It's a pity we're not in the same room,' Laila whispered in her ear. 'You know, I've never spent the night away from home.'

Zoe was actually happy they'd been given single rooms. She wanted to be alone and have some time to think about everything that happened during the day, about the new people, about all the new things she'd done and managed to prove to herself. She felt a bit sorry for Laila though, who seemed so terrified. Of course, Zoe knew that no one at school would ever have invited her to sleep over, or the other way round. But did that mean that Laila didn't even have any cousins that she'd stayed with, or family, friends, grandparents? Was that even possible?

The only thing to do was ask, she thought, even at

the risk of seeming nosy. If she was going to spend these two weeks with Laila, she might as well find out a bit more about her than the few tiny hints that filtered through her doll-like mask.

'Why's that then?' she finally asked her. 'How come you've never spent the night away from home?'

'Oh, well, you know, Mum gets anxious,' Laila explained, rummaging around in her flowery make-up bag. 'And all of our relatives live so far away. I mean, I've slept over at their places, of course, but it's always been the three of us. Me and Mum and Dad. I should probably be embarrassed that I've never had a sleepover at my age.' The way she said it, she sounded as though she was about thirty or forty, not twelve and a half. 'But the truth is . . .' she said, lowering her voice, 'no one's ever invited me. Not a friend, I mean.'

I can believe that, Zoe found herself thinking, but she managed not to say it out loud.

The flight attendant's voice interrupted the slightly embarrassed silence, announcing that the plane had started its descent: *Please put your seat in the upright position, fasten your seatbelt and stow your tray table for landing.* Laila held her breath, checked her belt, then sighed and leaned back in her seat. Zoe felt the tingle of excitement that she had whenever she was travelling somewhere and was about to arrive. It wasn't as though she'd done it that many times before, but the sensation was so clear and unmistakable. It was a mixture of anxiety and anticipation that had nothing to do with pure and simple fear: it was the same mixture of emotions that she felt when she was about to take on a new challenge. Sometimes she was surprised by how easy she found it to interpret the feelings that came from inside her. *Perhaps it's because I'm so used to listening to myself,* she thought. It certainly made things easier, anyway.

They looked out of the window and saw that they really were coming down fast now. They were looking down on mountains and green countryside filled with little meadows, trees and winding roads. You could even see sheep grazing down there. She could hardly believe that Milan could be so close. But it was! Milan, and all that it meant.

CHAPTER FOUR

Green Eyes

Zoe was a little disappointed to discover on the very first day of lessons that the summer course was actually a kind of huge, thorough, very detailed revision of things they'd already done. It was a bit like what happened before exams, when the barre suddenly became very important indeed and imagination had to give way to patience, concentration, precision, that kind of thing . . . She supposed that, even by Year Ten, the basic techniques of ballet could not be ignored. They had to be taken very seriously indeed. She couldn't help but complain a little to Gimenez at the end of three hours of *pliés* and *battements tendus*, which would be enough to last her for quite some time.

'This is a summer course to help you perfect your technique, Zoe,' Gimenez explained calmly. 'We're talking about classical dance. I know that it seems boring now. But I'm sure you'll feel the benefit when you are back at the Academy. Everything will seem so much easier. You still have plenty of time to study other things that might seem more exciting. How do you think you're going to throw yourself into modern dance, for example, if you haven't mastered the basics?'

Zoe thought she could hear Madame Olenska's brisk common sense in her words. Gimenez seemed so, so . . . unconventional, yes, that was the right word, but ultimately she believed in the rules, just like the headmistress. Of course, Zoe thought to herself, Madame Olenska wouldn't have chosen Gimenez as her substitute, then her assistant, if that hadn't been the case. Was the only original thing about Gimenez the bright red that she always flashed about, in her clothes and her make-up? Was that all?

Zoe had that thought, then instantly felt a bit mean. Gimenez really was a brilliant teacher and she was turning out to be a very good chaperone too. She went along to all of their lessons with Signor Rossi, a teacher who looked deceptively fragile, but who actually had muscles of steel and an eagle eye for the tiniest mistakes in posture. Gimenez helped them all out with a friendly smile, adding to what Signor Rossi had said for anyone who didn't understand his English (although he still called the positions by their French names), corrected their positions with incredible patience and then at the end of the lesson she stayed behind to explain any details that might have been lost in translation. Then, when classes were over for the day, she gave them almost unlimited freedom. They just had to return to the hotel in time to go out to dinner together, but until then they could go where they wanted as long as there were at least two of them, and as long as they were on foot – to make sure they didn't go far away from the school or the nearby hotel.

Anyway, as Leda had said, the school was in the centre of town, so there was no need to go far. There was more than enough going on nearby to keep them occupied. With Laila practically glued to her, holding on to her arm because she was scared of getting lost, Zoe wandered around the streets in the centre of Milan, past the cafés and restaurants and beautiful little boutiques. The most upmarket shopping area in town was quite close to the school and Zoe found it absolutely fascinating. The streets there were full of shops selling clothes by famous designers from Italy and all around the world. Zoe had seen some of the names in the fashion magazine that her mum's friend Alexa worked for. And in the centre of town there was the Galleria Vittorio Emanuele, a beautiful old shopping arcade, with a vaulted roof and a mosaic floor, and lots of nice little cafés and shops. One of the pictures in the floor mosaic was a bull and they said that if you spun around in a circle on the bull, it would bring you good luck. Zoe thought it'd be a lot nicer if there weren't quite so many tourists spinning and taking each other's photographs, but then she felt mean, because of course she was a tourist too. And Zoe noticed the local people seemed to like spinning on the bull as well. You could tell the Milanese just by looking at them. Even the ones who weren't very good-looking, which a lot of them were, still looked so smart and glamorous, with their perfectly groomed hair and their beautiful clothes and matching accessories. It was almost like being in a fashion show or a very stylish movie.

Zoe and Laila didn't talk very much as they walked around Milan. Zoe was wrapped up in her fantasies about fashion and films and there was a constant buzz of background noise that sounded so different, so foreign: even the city itself seemed to speak in a different language. Laila was wide-eyed at the sights as well and she forgot her nervousness in the excitement of the new city.

One evening they walked into a little courtyard, where a lot of elegant people in sharply cut clothes were drinking what looked like champagne. A very smart man, dressed all in black – black suit, black shirt, even a black tie – was checking names on a list and talking into a microphone that was clipped to the side of his head. Zoe was sure that some of the guests must be famous and she wanted to wait around to see if a film star was coming to the party, but she and Laila were so obviously out of place that they soon got waved away. Reluctantly, they left the courtyard and went back out on to the street, where limousines were pulling up and dropping off women in jewels and high heels and more men in smart suits. Zoe imagined how it might feel to be on the guest list one day, drinking champagne and wearing such beautiful clothes. She smiled to herself. It really sounded more like Leda's kind of thing.

Back in the real world, Zoe and Laila found a great shop that stocked the sort of clothes that Leda liked, and they went in so that Zoe could complete her mission and find Leda a violet top. She got a little sidetracked though, because she saw at least five things that she would have liked to buy for herself. Then she realised she still had a lot of time to go back, if she didn't find something she preferred in another shop.

Laila contemplated the jeans and the tiny little mini-skirts and tops and coloured cardigans with a look of enchantment on her face. 'I never buy clothes for myself,' she said very quietly while they were waiting in the queue to pay.

'You mean you haven't ever chosen anything for yourself? You can always start now. It's not that hard,' Zoe said, and she felt like such an expert. Then she remembered that it had been less than a year since she'd started buying clothes for herself.

'Now?' Laila asked, terrified. 'Maybe tomorrow.'

'Yes, tomorrow. Or another day,' Zoe replied, reassuring her. 'We've still got plenty of time.'

That was true, but it was deceptive too, because time always flies when you're away from home. *It's as though it goes at a different speed entirely,* thought Zoe one day, when she realised they were already halfway through the summer course. It seemed as though they'd only been there a day.

The hotel was very familiar now though, and really nice. The rooms were tiny, but comfortable. Zoe had a nice view out over the roofs and towers of Milan from her room, which was on the eighth floor. She'd already decided what she liked best for breakfast and really enjoyed starting the day with a proper Italian cappuccino with frothy milk on top and a pastry, preferably one with lots of gooey custard inside, although the ones with apricot jam in were pretty good too. The breakfast pastries looked almost identical, but Zoe had learned to tell them apart: the jam ones had a shiny top, the custard ones were covered in specks of icing sugar and the chocolate ones had little flakes of chocolate on top. Maybe it wasn't the healthiest of things to have for breakfast every day, but ballerinas do need a lot of energy, she reasoned, and this was almost a holiday, wasn't it?

At lunchtimes they ate in the ballet school canteen, which was just like school canteens all over the world – clean, but a little dreary, with everything tasting more or less the same.

Then, in the evenings, they went out with Gimenez to discover new places. Gimenez actually went beforehand to check out the restaurants and book in advance. They ate Japanese, Thai and, of course, lots of Italian food, which somehow tasted so much better than the pizza and pasta back home. Zoe also discovered that she really liked sushi.

'Yes, but what's the dance course like?' her dad had asked her one evening when she was enthusing about the city and the atmosphere and the shops and the food and the fantastic ice cream. They often spoke briefly on the phone, and they sent text messages, which she imagined flying over the mountains and across Europe and over the Channel. When things are going well you don't really have much to say to your family, but this was a longer phone call and her dad was keen to hear more details.

'Oh, the course. Fine, yes, no problems. You know, it's

a sort of revision course. It's not as though we're learning anything new,' she explained, with the experienced tone of voice that she'd copied from Gimenez. 'There are other groups of students here from schools all over Europe, but we only ever see them in the corridors. We don't have any lessons together.'

And that was a real shame, she thought after hanging up, because she'd seen a boy in the French group who looked a bit older than her, but not by too much. He seemed nice and he came to the classroom with his group after Zoe's group's lesson had finished. She always saw him waiting outside the room and he seemed to look out for her as well. She'd noticed that he had beautiful green eyes. He'd smiled at her the day before and she'd smiled back, and she thought she felt her heart beating faster.

How silly, she thought later when she was on her own. She'd always thought she wasn't the romantic, sentimental type at all. Maybe Green Eyes was really mean. How could you like a person you didn't know? Love at first sight? No, that was rubbish. That was just the kind of thing that happened in books and in films. Practical Zoe didn't recognise herself in this soppy, romantic Zoe who felt herself blush whenever Green Eyes looked at her, in those precious few seconds before he disappeared into Signor Rossi's clutches.

Zoe had investigated and found out that the French

group was staying in a small hotel right by the school – a kind of student hostel with dormitories of four or five beds. She had no idea where they went to eat in the evenings. She could wait until his lessons were over and tail him, or, more sensibly, she could actually talk to him and ask him what his name was. But, in the end, the thought that there was still so much of Milan to explore made her change her mind: why should she waste her few free hours chasing after someone she didn't even know?

So practical Zoe returned. After the lesson, she went back to the hotel for a shower and then hurried back out again. She and Laila had discovered a lovely little café on a small piazza with a fountain and cascades of geraniums. They sat at one of the tables outside and had a drink made from ice and lemon syrup. She'd had something like it at home before, but this felt much more sophisticated. It was so refreshing and cooling and Zoe thought how welcome it would be in the middle of one of Signor Rossi's dull stretching classes, which he was bound to be planning for the next day.

'It's fun being with you,' Laila said, between sips of her drink.

Zoe looked closely at Laila and noticed that she was looking unusually dishevelled. In their hurry to get out, she hadn't tidied the bun in her hair, so stray locks were bobbing around her cheeks and neck – a look she'd never seen on Laila before. She looked less like a doll and more like a real, live girl. Zoe suddenly had a radical idea. 'Laila, why don't you wear your hair down?'

'Down?' Laila looked at her, bewildered, as though she'd never even considered that possibility, which was probably true. 'Down?' she repeated, puzzled. '*Maman* says . . .'

'*Maman's* not here,' Zoe interrupted. 'Go on, just try it. I think it'd suit you.'

With a deep sigh, Laila picked up her glass, looked into it as though she thought she might find an answer at the bottom, drank the last few drops of icy syrup and put the glass down. Then she pulled out the grips that were holding her bun in place. Her hair tumbled down on to her shoulders, dark and glossy. Laila blushed. 'How do I look?'

'Come here,' Zoe said. She finished what was left of her drink and took Laila by the hand. It was a prickly hand, full of hairpins. She pulled her to the nearest shop, a shoe shop, full of the exquisite shoes that Milan is famous for, but Zoe wasn't interested in shoes this time. She pushed Laila over to a full-length mirror, then ruffled her hair a little to shake out the stiffness left behind by the hairgrips. 'There you go. See?'

Blushing even more now, Laila smiled nervously. She probably hardly recognised the Laila reflected in the mirror, captured within the glass, hesitating, before reaching up a hand to stroke the entire length of her beautiful mane.

'Promise me you'll keep it like that this evening,' Zoe said. 'And that you'll wear it that way whenever we go out.'

'Yes,' was all Laila said. And she smiled.

The transformation had begun.

CHAPTER FIVE

Butterflies

Signor Rossi was 'extremely satisfied' with the English group's performance and training. He never showed his enthusiasm in front of them, but he'd told Gimenez and she'd passed it on to them when they were in the changing rooms at the end of another barre lesson. One of the Year Ten girls, with pale golden hair and big blue eyes, remarked, a little wearily, 'There really was no need for him to tell us that. We know we're good.'

'Don't be so conceited, Jenny,' Gimenez replied, suddenly serious. 'The Academy is an excellent school, but perhaps you're forgetting that Signor Rossi is teaching a selection of the best students from schools all over Europe. The French group is exceptional. Truly exceptional. I stayed to watch one of their lessons. I don't think I have to remind you not to rest on your laurels. There's always someone somewhere who's better than you. Always.'

Jenny shrank under the weight of so many eyes staring at her, but she still tried to defend herself. 'But still, we are the best, aren't we?'

'Here? Now? Quite possibly, yes,' Gimenez admitted. 'But you've always got to work hard to stay the best and to keep on improving. There's always room for improvement.'

Zoe listened to the conversation, thinking how silly Jenny was being. She was the Laila of her class, ice-cold and perfect. Then she realised that she was actually being unfair to Laila. Maybe it was the new environment, perhaps being away from home, but since they'd arrived in Milan, Laila seemed like a new person. At least, she seemed more normal; she was still perfectly groomed, but without the aura of distance and the vague, superior smile that made her so unlovable. Zoe felt that she understood Laila a little better now that she knew her more. She was just serious and focused on what she was doing.

At dinner the evening before, everyone noticed Laila hadn't put her hair up. Gimenez was the first to comment. 'You look older, Laila,' she said.

Octavia, one of the Year Ten girls, added, 'When your hair's that beautiful, you should wear it loose on stage as well. You know, you can do that for certain parts. Alessandra Ferri wore her hair down when she danced Manon.'

'Oh, I don't think I could manage to be that dramatic,' Laila said, blushing.

'You should try,' Gimenez said to her. 'You might just surprise yourself.'

Before going to bed, Laila asked Zoe to come into her room, 'just for five minutes.' Their rooms were next door to each other. They weren't really supposed to – Gimenez was strict about bedtimes – but Zoe took a quick look down the corridor, saw there was no one else around, then slipped into Laila's room.

It was identical to her own room, except for the perfect tidiness, which almost made it look as though no one was using the room. The only traces of human activity were on the bedside table: a little pink bear in a tutu (the kind of thing that Zoe hated but Leda loved) and a tiny doll – the kind you find in a doll's house – also wearing a tutu. Zoe suddenly wondered whether there was such a thing as a doll's theatre, complete with stage, backdrop, wings and curtains, with tiny little people in evening dress in the audience.

'That's Emma,' Laila told Zoe, following her gaze. 'I've had her since I was four. She's my lucky mascot.

Would you like to take a look at her?' She picked up the doll and handed her to Zoe, with all the respect that is usually reserved for sacred objects.

Zoe looked at the fine brown hair, the heart-shaped red mouth, the slightly questioning eyes drawn on with black ink, the delicate tutu with a tiny edge of silver embroidery, and the little body, which was soft but strong beneath her fingers, just as a real ballerina's body should be. 'She's lovely,' she said finally.

'Do you really think I look good with my hair like this?' Laila asked her, abruptly changing subject.

'Yes,' Zoe said. 'Not because it makes you look older like Gimenez said, just because it makes you look . . . less . . . plastic.'

There, she'd said it. She waited for Laila's reaction. What if this new Laila, who seemed so vulnerable, just burst into tears? Why couldn't she have said 'less like a doll' or 'less perfect', or anything that didn't sound quite so offensive?

But Laila didn't cry and she didn't even look upset. In fact, she just looked curious, and she contemplated herself in the mirror as though she'd just discovered something that she wasn't previously aware of. Perhaps that was actually the case.

'You know,' she said, 'it's *Maman* who really likes my hair up. She says a ballerina shouldn't be like other girls. She has to be more serious.'

'What's your hair got to do with being serious?' Zoe asked.

'I don't know,' Laila admitted. 'I'm not really sure what she means.'

They didn't say anything else on the subject. Instead, Laila opened up the drawer of her bedside table and took out a little pink parcel. 'It's for you,' she said, handing the parcel to Zoe.

Zoe's first thought was, *But where did she get it? Did she bring it from home?* It was a fair assumption, because Laila had been glued to Zoe whenever they weren't at the school. Then Zoe remembered that she'd left Laila looking around one of the little shops by the Galleria that afternoon and Laila had caught up with her a few minutes later, out of breath as though she'd been running.

She opened the parcel. Inside was a small pink candle in a pink glass rose-shaped holder. The scent, of course, was also rose.

'It's because you've been so kind to me,' Laila said quietly. 'Even though I know I don't deserve it.'

Zoe knew very well what Laila was talking about: the endless series of spiteful remarks, cruel jokes, and general nastiness that had marked their shared history at the Academy. The time they'd been forced to spend together had been full of nasty insults and open hostility.

'We were only little,' Zoe said. 'We've both grown up now. Let's just forget about it. Thank you for the gift.' She wasn't sure what to do next. If Leda had given her a present, she'd have hugged her to say thank you. But Laila wasn't Leda and she wasn't really her friend. So instead she just smiled and wished Laila goodnight.

Later, after she'd sneaked back to her own room without getting caught by Gimenez and put her very pink candle on the bedside table, Zoe threw herself on to the bed and thought about how strange things can be and how things change. About how, for a long time, she'd felt so distant from Leda, who had always been her best friend, and about how they'd become close again, so naturally. About Sara, and how difficult it was to have a close relationship with a big sister – sometimes their relationship looked like a temperature chart for someone with a fever, all ups and downs. And about how Laila might actually be shaking off her doll-like perfection. It seemed even more impossible to believe that Zoe was the person Laila might finally be opening up to. They'd never made a secret of the fact that they didn't like each other. And finally she thought about how happy she was to be surrounded by the delicate scent of rose that was spreading through the darkness of the room, a sweet and familiar fragrance that still had a touch of something new.

Another new thing was the bundle of emotions she'd been carrying around since that morning, when

Green Eyes had spoken to her. 'My name's André. What's yours?' he'd said, in English with a lovely French accent.

Zoe told him.

'Ah, Zoe,' he'd repeated. 'See you around?'

Zoe nodded, relieved to find out that his English was okay. Then it was time for her class to go in. They could already hear Signor Rossi's stick banging on the floor, up and down like a piston, which was how he summoned his flock. He sometimes called them his 'little sheep' when he was in a very good mood. He probably thought it was a compliment.

'See you around,' André had said. But what did he mean exactly?

The French group's accompanying teacher was a man with a strange little devilish beard that tapered into two sideburns that looked as though they were drawn on his cheeks. He never smiled. Zoe would have hated a teacher like that. Gimenez was a thousand times nicer. Zoe doubted that 'Monsieur Devil' would let his students roam around as they pleased. One of André's classmates had told Olivia in Year Ten that they were only allowed to go out with him and that he took them to see churches and monuments and dull stuff like that.

She guessed that André would just remain a name (it was a nice name, though) linked to the memory of a special trip. Zoe felt a bit guilty, because when she was thinking about him, Roberto's friendly face, with his red hair and his curious lack of freckles, popped into her mind, uninvited. They hadn't seen each other much before school finished for the summer, using the excuse of work for the end-of-year exams. But it did seem exactly that – an excuse. They'd gone out for a meal before he left, and texted a lot since then, but that was all.

'It's only natural, Zoe, at your age,' her mum had said when Zoe had confided in her about her worries and confusion. 'You should be out there enjoying yourself and trying new things.'

Zoe, who was usually rather cautious by nature, suddenly wanted to start experiencing life right now, and doing something braver than just sneaking into another room after lights out. She was enjoying the freedom and slightly nervous excitement of being away from home, and she wondered what Milan might be like at night, with all those models and film stars and lights and glamour . . . But then again, it was probably just like any other big city and it would have been dangerous to go out alone, but that wasn't really what was on Zoe's mind. She was thinking how nice it would be to go out with André, to take him by the hand and go and visit the sights that were now so familiar to her, and see how different they looked at night. That would be a great adventure, wouldn't it?

Maybe, she thought, it was the kind of adventure that was only fun when it was in your head. And maybe André only seemed so appealing because she didn't really know him.

'That's true,' said a little voice in her head. 'But if you don't get to know him, how will you ever find out for sure?'

CHAPTER SIX

A Visit

Out of the blue, as though summoned by her thoughts, Roberto called Zoe while they were having breakfast the following morning.

'Are you free this evening?' Roberto asked. 'My mum and dad would like to take us both out for dinner.'

'I think . . . I'll have to ask Gimenez,' she said, and she did so straightaway. Gimenez was happy to give her permission, because she knew Roberto and his family so well.

When Laila heard the news, she looked a little upset, but then she said, 'Never mind, I'll just stay in the hotel and read for a bit.'

Olivia, who had heard everything, said, 'Why don't

you come out with us? We're going to the cinema with Gimenez. It's just around the corner.' So Zoe was relieved that Laila had something fun to do too.

Having spoken to Roberto, Zoe felt even more confused about André than before. When he walked past them in the corridor, he nodded at her, the way boys do, and all the girls laughed. When they got to the changing rooms, one of the older girls said, 'Ooh, making foreign conquests, eh?' and everyone burst out laughing again.

Another of the girls, who had heard the conversation with Gimenez at breakfast that morning, said, 'You reckon? She's practically engaged. Her boyfriend's even followed her all the way over here. It's official. They're actually going out with Mummy and Daddy tonight.'

Zoe didn't say anything, but just looked away and concentrated on getting changed. Anyway, she wasn't exactly offended. Why should she be? In fact, she was rather pleased that she had *two* boys interested in her.

She took particular care when she was getting ready that night, and decided to wear her new green striped top for the first time, which she'd bought in a shop near the school.

She wondered about taking a cardigan. It was surprising how quickly the temperature could change. The black one would do.

Zoe wasn't sure she liked Laila's lip-gloss, but Laila

had insisted on lending it to her.

She sent her mum a text message. *Having fun. Love Z.* She knew her mum would say it was too short, but what was she supposed to say? *Don't know if I really want to see R?*

And she really didn't know whether she wanted to see him, but now that he was there in the hotel lobby, and he got up from the grey sofa where he'd been waiting, and came over to her and kissed her on the cheek, she had to admit that she was happy to see him. She thought he seemed a bit taller now and he looked really good in the clothes he was wearing. She couldn't help but notice his look of surprise and admiration when he saw her, which was the best way of telling her, without actually saying so, that she looked good too – maybe even better than he remembered. His parents were there, and as lovely as ever, but his little brother wasn't – he was too young to stay up late at night. It was a pity, thought Zoe, because he'd have filled any awkward silences.

In the end, though, everything went fine. Roberto's parents had chosen a nice little restaurant in one of the side streets in the area with all of the designer shops. It was typically Italian and very elegant, with crisp white tablecloths and old-fashioned waiters who smiled a lot and said '*Molto bene*' when you ordered something, just as though you'd chosen the very thing they would have picked themselves if they'd been ordering.

After a brief exchange of information about how everyone was and what they'd all been up to, Roberto's mum and dad got really wrapped up in a conversation about their planned trip to America. To start with, it was good fun, but as they became bogged down in details, Zoe began to lose interest. She glanced over at Roberto and could see that he was feeling the same way. With a sort of unspoken agreement, they started talking about other things.

They'd already talked about the classes at the summer course and how Roberto's mum had been a little disappointed that he hadn't been chosen to take part. They'd talked about Gimenez and Zoe had told them about Signor Rossi and made them laugh, and she'd even told them all about the new, improved Laila, which resulted in amazement all round. Everyone at the Academy knew everything about everyone else, and that included the parents, because the Academy was more than just a school – it was a place where their children worked hard and dreamed about their futures.

Now, as she sank her fork into the delicious rolls of aubergine and ricotta that she'd ordered as a starter, Zoe waited for Roberto to ask her something a little more private and maybe rather uncomfortable – something she wouldn't know how to answer, something that would embarrass her and force her to fill her mouth as quickly as possible so she would have a good reason not to answer. But he just looked at her and said what she'd already seen in his eyes. 'You look good. You seem happy.'

'Yes, yes, I think I am,' Zoe replied calmly.

'I've been feeling a bit down. After school finished, we just headed off to Italy and there wasn't even any time to . . . you know . . . patch things up properly.'

At that point Zoe felt she should have said there was no patching up to do, because everything was wonderful, and she imagined that if they were in a film, that would have been the right response. She'd have gently blushed and he'd have taken her hand and raised it to his lips and *CUT!* But that wasn't what she wanted to say. What she wanted to say was, 'Well, maybe it's just as well,' so that's exactly what she said.

'What do you mean?' Suddenly, Roberto looked pale and serious. He looked at Zoe as though he didn't understand.

She sighed. It would be nice to be silent now, just to concentrate on the delicious food. She thought that maybe she'd have just a little space left for a light and refreshing sorbet afterwards. If they had to talk, she wished it could be about fun and trivial things, like all of the lovely shops nearby and the holiday she was going on with her family and a bit of gossip about the Year Tens. But no. She had to be honest with him. So Zoe found herself saying, with a calmness that was at odds with the way she felt inside, 'You know, after everything that happened . . . I . . . I'm not annoyed with you anymore. I got over it a while ago. But maybe it's too soon for us to be together like that. I want us to keep on going out together – you, me, Leda and Lucas, and maybe other people too. You know, as a bunch of friends. I'm not saying I want a new boyfriend.'

'No, I know,' said Roberto softly. 'I realised that when I made such an idiot of myself over Alex. I mean, I know you'd say if there was someone else. And I know that it's my fault you're telling me these things now. I got things completely out of proportion and I can't say it often enough: I am sorry. You don't know how much I'd give to go back to the way we were before. It was so good.'

'That's true,' Zoe said. 'But, you know, what we had was fun and no one can change that. It's something we'll always share.' And she saw that Roberto cheered up instantly. 'But we have changed. Or things have changed. We're not the same people we were before. We can't be.'

Roberto looked serious again. 'You're right,' was all he said. 'So there's no hope for me?'

Zoe smiled. Roberto sounded so dramatic. 'Come on, Roberto,' she said. 'I said we should carry on seeing each other in a group. I like you. You know I do. And we'll see how things go.'

'We'll see,' he repeated, with a sigh. 'Zoe, Zoe . . .'

'Maybe when you see Laila again in September you'll

fall down at her feet,' she joked, to lighten the atmosphere.

'Yeah, right,' he replied. 'Like that's going to happen.'

'Like that's going to happen,' she said, imitating him. 'Don't be too hasty. Never say never.'

'You've seen too many films,' he said.

'So have you,' she replied. 'Dozens and dozens of those soppy love films that they have on TV all summer in the afternoon.'

'And what's so bad about that? Is romance just for girls?'

The two of them laughed together, friends again. At least they had that. Then their starters were cleared away, and moments later plates of steaming golden saffron risotto arrived.

For a while, they just ate and that was enough. Then, after the waiter brought Zoe's sorbet – two balls of pale yellow icy lemon with a sprig of mint – they started to chat again, between spoonfuls of dessert. And as the sharp taste of lemon flooded her tongue, Zoe found herself thinking about how much fun she was having, and how simple and easy everything could be with Roberto; they could leave behind all the complicated stuff, just shrug it all off, like a rucksack that had become too heavy.

She felt calm, relaxed, like when . . . like when you spend time with a friend. Suddenly it all became clear.

Roberto was a friend. She couldn't say he was 'just' a friend, because that would be spoiling something special. But that was how it was. He had to learn to accept it. And who knew? Maybe when he went on his mammoth trek across America, he might meet some beautiful Californian surfer girl who danced in an avant-garde dance company and who needed someone to create a dance just for her. *Would I be jealous?* Zoe wondered. And she answered herself: *No, I wouldn't.* There was room for lots of people in a friendship. It was like a boat made of rubber, which expanded to fit everyone who got on. That was a nice image, she thought. She could go to bed happy now.

And so she did. After saying goodnight to Roberto and his parents in the hotel lobby, she headed upstairs and told Gimenez she was back, as they'd agreed. Zoe fell asleep almost as soon as her head hit the pillow. It was time to dream and to process the events of the day. She couldn't remember what she'd dreamed about when she woke the next day, but there was a smile on her lips and she felt the calmness of someone who has clear thoughts in her mind and pleasant memories in her heart.

CHAPTER SEVEN

Discoveries

'Please, Laila, that's enough. Come on, let's go.' Zoe meant it to come across as a threat, but it lost some force because she was forced to whisper it in Laila's ear. It didn't achieve the desired result. Laila was determined to stay until the end of the puppet show that she was enjoying, along with a crowd of young spectators. Laila stood there in her neat, blue pleated skirt (okay, so her style still needed a little more work), a top identical to the one that Zoe had bought for Leda, and turned-down ankle socks which disappeared into a fun pair of pink trainers.

Zoe took a step backwards to enjoy the scene. It was

really sweet somehow, but also kind of bizarre. Laila with her hair down and that strange combination of clothes – it was such a new and daring look for her. The puppets were having a fight and it was funny watching Laila trying to understand the jokes and then laughing just a split second after the Italian children.

'Let's go,' Zoe repeated to her. 'You know we're going to the theatre tonight.'

'I'm already at the theatre,' Laila retorted.

Oh no, thought Zoe, *now she thinks she's a comedian.* 'But we've still got to have a shower and we're supposed to be meeting Gimenez in half an hour . . .'

This time it worked. Laila gasped. 'Half an hour? I'll never dry my hair in time.'

She managed, just. They all got to the lobby on time, fresh from the shower and ready to venture out into the Milan evening, to go and see some of the best dancers in Italy performing. Dancing for the ballet company in Milan was a dream for many young ballerinas, including Zoe. Some of the dancers from Milan had visited the Academy once, a few years ago, and everyone had fallen in love with them.

Zoe wasn't the type to put posters on her wall or collect autographs or that kind of thing. She'd always been quite subtle about her passion, but she was a regular visitor to the website of the Milan dance company and she usually knew what they were dancing each season and who the principal dancers were. They were dancing a new ballet this evening and, even though it was officially sold out, Gimenez had managed to get tickets for all of them through one of her contacts.

The group all left for the theatre together and it felt strange, because it was the first time since they'd arrived in Milan ten days before that they'd really done something as a group like that. Even when they went out to dinner together, Gimenez booked separate small tables for them and they split up into little groups, rather than booking a huge table. They preferred not to stand out too much, but there was no way to avoid it that evening.

Laila and Zoe walked a little apart from the rest of the group. Gimenez kept turning round to check that they were all still there. She wasn't really worried about them, but just a little concerned that something – someone taking a wrong turn, someone popping into a shop to buy sweets and not coming out quickly enough – might spoil the evening's fun. Sasha, one of the Year Tens, came over to them and started chatting. 'Isn't it nice being away from home? All this freedom . . . I'd like to stay here forever. I tell you, as soon as I've done all my exams, I want to leave home, do all the auditions I can find all over the world and hope that someone out there wants me. I can't wait!'

Laila looked at Sasha and said to her, 'Yes, that's

exactly what I want to do too.'

There was a really nice atmosphere in the group. Everyone knew it wasn't really school and no one was in competition with anyone else, only with themselves. The point of the summer course was to improve without having to win or to pass exams or anything. Zoe thought that must be the reason why even the older girls, who seemed so high and mighty at school that they were almost like alien beings, were just ordinary people here. They were a few years older and a bit more experienced as dancers, but not all that different really.

Their class didn't have any boys in it, which seemed a bit strange. The few boys who had been in the class had fallen by the wayside, so when they did *pas de deux* they had to borrow boys from the older classes, which had its advantages, as Leda often pointed out. When all of them were together like that, they looked like a gaggle of girls from one of those films about boarding schools. All that was missing was the uniforms.

Zoe looked at Laila curiously. She'd always thought that Laila defended her territory at the Academy because she thought it was hers and she didn't want anyone to be as good as her on her home turf. The thought of a Laila who was able to go out into the world and face its challenges was another new thing.

What was she going to tell Leda when she went home and her friend saw that she was on friendly terms with their despised classmate? Zoe wasn't really worried about it. While Leda appeared to be naturally suspicious and full of prejudices, she was also very quick to accept changes. It wouldn't surprise Zoe if Leda ended up seeing Laila as a difficult patient for whom a cure had finally been found, but who still had a long period of rehabilitation and therapy ahead of her.

Eleanor, another Year Ten, came over to join the three of them. She must have been listening to them, because she said, 'Can you imagine how much you'd miss your family though?' They all nodded, because even if they were ballerinas, they were still rather young ballerinas.

'Here we are!' Gimenez said, waving a leaflet so that they'd look at her, but there was really no need, because her bright-red dress was impossible to ignore. She certainly stood out in the crowd. Gimenez wasn't the only one of them who looked elegant that night, though. Everyone had felt the need to dress up for the ballet, and even though there were lots of pairs of jeans, the top halves were all pretty cardigans and sparkly tops.

Lots of people turned round to look at them in the foyer of the theatre. *We are quite a sight,* Zoe thought, as she saw their group's multiple reflections in the mirrors lining the entrance. For some reason, she'd expected a huge theatre. It was smaller than she'd imagined, but lavishly decorated, like an exquisite jewellery box, and the staff were wearing uniforms that were smart and covered with braid so that they almost looked like theatrical costumes. Gimenez saw Zoe looking around and came over to her. 'It's not as big as you expected, eh? But this building's full of history. And look at those painted ceilings and chandeliers!'

They hardly had any time to get a proper look at the theatre before they had to go into the auditorium. The lights went down, the conductor came in, bowed to the audience and the curtains slowly slid aside.

It was such a special evening. It was amazing to see the dancers. They were so skilled and the girls were able to appreciate more than the rest of the audience just how much work went into making the steps look so effortless. It was an extraordinary combination of strength and grace, which every ballerina needs to have, but these dancers somehow had something extra, something that set them apart from ordinary dancers, something that all of the Academy girls hoped to learn for themselves. These dancers showed not a trace of fragility, sentimentality or weakness.

The set was very simple, based around moving lights, which glowed, then faded. The costumes were very basic leotards, all designed to emphasise the perfect gestures and movements.

It was so beautiful. Zoe couldn't exactly say why. She'd seen many dance performances, of all different kinds, and she knew that not everyone shared her passion. Even some of her schoolmates who loved to dance themselves didn't really like watching it. But Zoe loved looking at dance, partly because of Lucas, who was so mad about contemporary dance, and also because of Roberto, who wanted to be a choreographer when he was older. They both had a different way of looking at things. Zoe felt she could really appreciate what she was seeing.

When it came to the interval, though, Laila couldn't stop talking. She'd only ever seen very classical ballets with the most traditional choreography, she explained excitedly, and she had no idea that dance could be like this too. After talking so much, she suddenly fell silent and slumped against the back of her seat as though she were overwhelmed.

Zoe smiled at her. 'It's a nice surprise, then?'

Laila just nodded, lost in her thoughts about what she'd seen, clearly replaying it again and again in her imagination. When the lights went down again, she sat up straight, her eyes gleaming, ready to enjoy the spectacle once more.

When it was over, they all chatted as they left the building, exchanging opinions and thoughts about what they'd seen. Zoe found herself talking to Anita, a girl she hardly knew. She was slim, dark-haired and tall. She'd decided that when she grew up she was going to do experimental dance – something exciting that had never been done before. She described her plans as 'experiments with the body'.

'Did you see that Spanish dancer, Joaquin whatever-his-name-was?' Nadia cheerfully interrupted them, as she caught up with them. 'Oh, you two are so serious. Can't talk to you about boys, I can see that. But he was so gorgeous . . .'

'He *was* so gorgeous? I'd say he still is. Look over there,' Anita said to her, laughing. He must have got changed in a flash, because Joaquin the dancer was already leaving by the stage door, where a girl with a cloud of blond hair was waiting for him. She dived into his arms. 'It would seem that he's taken.'

'Hmm, that figures, I guess,' Nadia said, studying the two of them with great interest, as were all of the other girls. It was such a beautiful scene, the reunion of the tired and contented artiste and his lover.

'Stop staring at them like that. The show's over. We're the ones who'll look like fools if they notice us,' Anita hissed.

So, with giggles and whispers, the girls walked out into the night, which was illuminated with hundreds of streetlights, lights from houses and buildings and shop windows, with a soundtrack of cars and voices and unfamiliar sounds. Gimenez seemed less like a chaperone on a school trip now. She was relaxed and happy, almost like a big sister. She said goodnight to them in the lobby. 'It was a very special evening for me,' she added. 'I hope it was for you too.'

Soon afterwards, in the corridor outside their rooms, Laila whispered to Zoe, 'It was a very special evening for me too. Wonderful. Thank you.'

'But I didn't do anything,' Zoe said.

'Oh, no. You did a lot. Maybe not this evening. But you've done a lot.' With that, she disappeared into her room.

Thinking about it afterwards, Zoe realised that Laila wasn't exaggerating. She'd told the truth. Zoe knew that she could have continued to be hostile to her proud, doll-like classmate, or maybe just indifferent, but instead she'd shown patience and allowed Laila to spend time with her, even giving up some of her precious independence so that Laila would feel less uncomfortable in this situation that was so new to her. The point was that she'd done it because she'd wanted to, and she'd enjoyed it. So was it necessary for Laila to thank her? Maybe that didn't matter. What mattered was that she felt good and so did Laila. Sometimes it really didn't take much to make you feel good.

CHAPTER EIGHT

Back Home

'You have to tell me everything, and I mean absolutely everything. Is one evening going to be enough?'

Zoe was at Leda's house. She was looking at Zoe with hunger in her eyes, as though Zoe was a tasty dish that was waiting to be eaten up. She was expecting lots of gossip from her friend after two weeks away in Milan. Of course, she'd put on her Italian top straightaway.

'We'll make sure it's enough,' Zoe said with a smile, as she threw herself back on to the pile of soft cushions in assorted shades of pink that covered her friend's bed. They were having a sleepover and it was going to be the last time they'd see each other for a while, because Leda was going on holiday to the seaside with her mum the next day, and when she got back, Zoe would have already gone on her family holiday. They wouldn't see each other until the beginning of September, just before school started.

So that they wouldn't miss each other too much, they'd worked out a plan for swapping messages – emails, texts and even hand-written letters. Leda was going through a writing phase, thanks to the beautiful paper that she'd been given as an end-of-term present, which she'd decided to put to good use as soon as she could. In the meantime, they were taking the opportunity to talk.

Zoe told Leda all about the new, improved Laila. Leda was sceptical to start with, but Zoe managed to convince her and she also explained her own theory, which was so simple it was almost dull: years of isolation 'partly self-inflicted, of course' and too much mollycoddling had turned Laila into the mechanical doll they all knew – self-confident to a fault, conceited and a know-it-all. This was also partly because she had genuine and undeniable skill. All it took was for Laila to leave her familiar surroundings for a while and encounter the big, wide world to reveal how fragile she was. Instead of shutting herself away, as she could have done, she simply asked for help. And Zoe gave it to her, and that was that. You didn't have to be physically close to be friendly, but friendships could sometimes follow.

'We'll see what it's like when we get back to school,' Leda said. 'She's got weeks and weeks to go back to the way she was.'

They forgot about the subject for a while and Zoe told Leda about Roberto, about her own doubts and how they'd decided, more or less together (she fibbed a bit about that) to be friends.

'It's such a shame,' Leda sighed. 'You were so good together.'

'But I just told you we're going to carry on seeing each other, just not on our own but with you, with Lucas, with Alissa . . .'

'Ah, speaking of Alissa, did you know she came over here to stay the night last week? I'm just mentioning it so that you don't find out from her and get annoyed with me. We had fun. We watched two DVDs, until one in the morning, and stuffed our faces with popcorn. I felt sick all the next day.'

'Nice one,' Zoe said, laughing. 'I hope Alissa felt better than you did.'

'It was sweet popcorn with butter,' Leda added, guiltily. 'I have to say, it was pretty good. Want to try some?'

'It's making me feel queasy just listening to you describe it!' Zoe said. 'But if you happen to have a bit of ice cream . . .'

They continued the conversation over two overflowing bowls of chocolate chip ice cream.

'Blah, blah, blah,' interrupted Leda eventually. 'You keep avoiding the most important subject. You still haven't told me anything about your little Frenchman.'

'Oh, that's so mean! Little Frenchman? What are you on about? That's not how you'd describe someone who's taller than us, is it?'

'And he's only fifteen. He's still growing!'

'Yes, but I can't imagine he'd get any cuter than he already is.'

'You're right, the older people get, the worse they look. It's enough of a miracle that he wasn't covered in spots.'

'You're such an idiot sometimes.'

'We've discussed this issue on several occasions and we both know it's true, so don't try to change the subject. I want you to tell me seriously . . .'

Zoe, faking a reluctance she really didn't feel at all, finally told Leda about André. About how one evening she'd bumped into him outside the hotel, coming back from a delicious Chinese meal. About how all the other girls had giggled a little, but been kind enough to give them some privacy, and how he'd casually asked her if she wanted to go out to a café for a quick drink. Zoe looked over at Gimenez, and she nodded back at her with a quick twitch of her lips, which Zoe interpreted as

'Fine, as long as you're not back too late.' And so, perched on the leather stools of a café, beneath the low-hanging lights, with a big glass of tonic water with a slice of lemon on the side, Zoe and André finally talked.

His English was pretty good, and with a few French words and a little hesitation, he told her it was the first time he'd been selected to do a summer course and he was really pleased. She found out that he lived in a small town and so he'd had to leave his home and his family to live at the school where he studied, that the distance was hard sometimes, but that he had quite a lot of friends and that helped.

Then she told him her story, feeling very lucky because she could study at the Academy without having to be apart from her mum and her dad and her sisters, something she'd never really thought about seriously until she spoke to him about it. Then she told him about Laila, about the problems they'd had and the recent changes, about her friends at home, and they talked about films and books. They talked about Signor Rossi and his peculiarities, about his way of saying 'higher, higher, higher', or 'like that, like that, like that', repeating everything three times, always, always, always.

'All that conversation in one evening?' Leda asked, a little concerned. 'I bet you didn't get to bed until three.'

'No, no,' Zoe said. 'We went out again.'

'You mean you met up on other evenings?'

'Well, we didn't have that many evenings left,' Zoe said with a smile.

'Did he take you out for a meal?'

'No, Gimenez had already been pretty generous letting me see him every evening until we left anyway, so I don't think she was going to let me skip meals with the rest of the group. But the last evening, André and I stayed up talking in the hotel until midnight.'

'Did you always go to the same café?'

'Yes, every time. Fortunately, we were usually the only ones there.'

'Did he kiss you?'

'Yes. On the cheek, when we said goodbye.'

'Oh,' Leda said. She sounded disappointed.

'Come on, what did you expect?'

'Oh, I don't know. A touch of passion would have been nice. Someone gets to know a handsome French dancer with green eyes, who is obviously veeeery interested in her, and it all ends with a peck on the cheek?'

'Maybe you're forgetting one thing,' Zoe said.

'Like what?'

'Like I'm hardly ready for a steady boyfriend.'

'Yes you are!'

'He's fifteen.'

'Oh, whatever. Do you know what? I envy you. You've had this wonderful romantic experience in a big

European city while you were doing this high-flying dance course. It's almost like being in a film. But I hate you too. You're just so laid back, the way you talk about it, sitting there with your arms behind your head, as if you were telling me you'd been out to do the shopping with your mum.'

Leda picked up a little cushion and threw it at Zoe, who grabbed it in midair, hugged it and laughed.

'Did you at least feel sad when you had to say goodbye?' Leda asked.

'Of course I did. But we'll keep in touch.'

'There you go, all we were missing was the story of impossible love and two lovers separated by hundreds of miles. Maybe now you'll stop eating, and cry over him every night, because all you can think about is him . . . But what am I saying? That's what I'd do. You're not made the same way. Look at you, lying there, completely calm, relaxed . . . Ooooh, I hate you, Zoe.'

They laughed together, then Zoe suddenly went serious. She looked at her friend and said, 'I forgot to tell you the most important thing.'

'Let me guess. André is coming to study at the Academy. André has a gorgeous twin brother who wants to meet me. André doesn't exist, he's a figment of your imagination. Or you just invented it all because you didn't have anything interesting to tell me and you knew I wasn't going to put up with that.'

'Yeah, right. No, this really is important. Look . . .' She took a top out of her overnight bag – a violet one identical to the one she'd bought for Leda and that Leda was now wearing. 'I decided to follow a trend for once. I thought it might be nice to play at being twins.'

She slipped it on over her white vest. Leda and Zoe looked at each other, then stood up and walked together to the full-length mirror that Leda had insisted on having in her room, which always made Zoe think of a princess's bed chamber. The splash of violet seemed to suit both of the girls in different ways. Maybe it was because they were happy and they were such good friends, but it felt just right.

'Do you really have to go away tomorrow?' Zoe said to Leda, a little later, once the lights were off.

'What about you, do you really have to be away for the only three days I'll be back in town before I go away again?'

'Maybe it'll do us good to spend some time apart,' Zoe said, seriously, in the same tone of voice that couples use when they're discussing their relationship.

Leda spotted the joke straightaway and declared, 'If you're planning to dump me, I think it would be best to tell me straight out.'

Zoe smiled in the dark and then a thought suddenly occurred to her. 'Let's be serious for a moment. Listen, what if, one day, you and I have a proper argument and we really do fall out and grow apart?'

'We'll always have the memories,' Leda replied, with a giggle. Then she added, 'I think I can rule that out. You know my mum and her best friend, Paula? They've known each other since they were at primary school. So, maybe it's a genetic thing. That's the way friendship works in my family. Okay? So don't go getting any silly ideas about leaving me. I'm already worried enough about this thing with Laila. Do you think she's going to hang around with us all the time?'

'You'll see. You're going to like her. She doesn't have a clue what to wear. You'll have an opportunity to do a total make-over.'

'Hmm, with that pretty little face of hers made up in the right way and the right clothes, we could do great things.'

'Exactly. We could transform her. Or at least, complete the transformation. Then her mum won't even let her in the house because she won't recognise her.'

'A friendly Laila with a smile on her face, maybe even making jokes, wearing jeans and trainers. Oh, the shock! The horror!'

Two knocks – and the bedroom door opened. 'Girls, are you still awake? Do you know what time it is?' asked Leda's mum.

'Why are you still awake, Mum?' teased Leda. 'Do

you know what time it is? And you've got a four-hour drive tomorrow!'

'You're right. I'm off to bed. You too, ladies, off to sleep.'

The door closed, and Zoe thought how good it felt to be home, falling asleep with her best friend beside her. She felt so lucky to have a lovely family, friends, to be able to dance, to meet new people . . .

Zoe stayed awake for a while, thinking about André and how, now that she'd told someone about it, it all seemed a bit more real. Those evenings perched on the high stools, choosing a different drink every time, drawing patterns on the tall misted glasses . . . Every time they'd said goodbye and she'd walked across the lobby, gone up in the lift and pushed the door to her room closed with her shoulder, she'd felt as though she'd imagined it all. Even though they'd struggled a bit to communicate, she felt totally relaxed with André, and had found it really exciting to be with him. But, as Leda had complained, there'd been nothing more than that. They didn't need anything else though. It had already been extraordinarily extraordinary as it was, especially special. That alone had been enough to make the summer course in Milan a memorable event.

Leda hadn't noticed, and she wasn't really interested anyway, but Zoe had only told her the bare minimum about the summer course itself: we did this and that, the teacher was strict, but okay, and that was it. If Zoe were to bump into Madame Olenska on the street – which was unlikely, but not impossible, particularly because she had to go into town with her mum to do a bit of last-minute shopping before going on holiday – she certainly couldn't stand there telling her about the exact shade of green of André's eyes. She'd have to manage to make at least one insightful comment about Signor Rossi's methods. But at that moment the lessons seemed so distant in her memory that she fell asleep before she could come up with anything appropriate to say.

CHAPTER NINE

A Private Rehearsal

'How did the fond farewells go? It must have been such a traumatic scene, with Leda leaning out of the car window in floods of tears. Or am I wrong?' Lucas asked.

'Oh, you're pretty close,' Zoe said with a laugh.

She and Lucas were on their usual bench in the park, with their feet where their bums should be and their bums a little higher on the backrest. They actually saw it as their bench, so they felt perfectly entitled to sit there like that, even when an old lady went past muttering something about young people today and no one teaching them decent behaviour, so it was no wonder they were making the seat all dirty with their feet. They didn't pay any attention to her, but looked at each other with raised eyebrows.

In actual fact, Leda's departure had been almost painless. Both of them had been too sleepy for any real emotions to surface, so they just gave each other a hug, like a couple of happy sloths. Zoe had woken up a bit more by the time she got home and she hurried out to look for Lucas so that she wouldn't start to feel down in the dumps. It was exactly the right thing to do, because they were now laughing and joking around, like the two friends they were, and, combined with a couple of cans of fizzy drink, it was a perfect way to deal with the early afternoon heat.

'Good, isn't it?' Lucas said, taking another swig. 'Dad says everyone used to drink this stuff when he was little, but then you couldn't find it for ages. I'm glad someone decided to start making it again. Most fizzy drinks are too sweet for this kind of weather.'

'That's true,' Zoe agreed. 'I really like proper homemade iced tea and lemonade too. The way people used to make it in the old days. Without any artificial flavourings.'

'How long is it before you and Leda see each other again? Six weeks? Do you think you'll survive? No, that's a silly question. Of course you'll survive. I'm a bit worried about Leda though.'

'Ah, listen to that. You're worried about Leda. That's got to mean something,' Zoe said, looking at Lucas expectantly. Leda really hadn't said very much on the subject.

'I'd leave that subject well alone if I were you,' warned Lucas. 'Every time we went out together, we managed to find at least one good reason to have an argument. See, we don't really like the same things. She's bored by the stuff I like, especially my taste in music. And I can't stand those soppy films she likes. One time I actually fell asleep and she got really upset. But it was towards the end. I'd seen almost the whole film, so I knew how it was going to end.'

'So what's going on with the two of you?'

'Nothing. We weren't going out with each other before and we aren't going out with each other now. She's great as a friend, but that's it. And when the autumn comes, we can all be a nice little gang again.'

'Have you spoken to Roberto?'

'We've talked on the phone a couple of times. I know all about it. You don't have to tell me anything.'

'I wasn't intending to.'

'I think the two of us agree on this subject, then,' he said, smiling. 'Just forget about love and all that kind of thing. Let's have fun and leave it at that. Right?'

Zoe nodded. She could hardly believe she'd not had to give any explanations. Now they could talk about other things.

'Hey, look over there,' said Lucas. 'It's Laila! What's she doing here?'

Zoe followed Lucas's gaze. He was staring at Laila, who was walking towards them.

'All alone too. Now that I think about it,' he continued, 'I've never seen her outside of school without her mum before.' He paused. 'Does she look different to you? What's she done to her hair?'

'Nothing,' Zoe said. 'It's just that she's wearing it down, that's all.'

'That's it? Are you sure? She looks like a different person.'

'In a way, maybe she is,' Zoe felt like saying, but she decided to keep quiet. It was better to let Lucas find out for himself.

'Hi,' Laila said, stopping in front of Zoe and Lucas. She held a hand above her eyes so that she could see them through the glare of the sun. 'Am I late?'

'No,' Zoe said, 'we haven't been here long.'

Lucas looked at Zoe with an obvious question on his face: *Did you actually arrange to meet her here?*

Laila obviously didn't know quite what to say, or what to do, let alone where to put her hands and feet. She shifted her weight from one foot to the other and slipped her hands into her jeans pockets. *Jeans?* thought Zoe. *Where did those come from? She didn't have them in Milan.* Then Laila took her hands out of her pockets and clasped her hands in front, then crossed her arms behind her back, nervous and uncertain. Zoe really felt for her and, to save her from the embarrassment, she decided to do the talking, to say what Laila wanted to say.

'Lucas,' she began, 'Laila would like to ask you a favour. We went to see a show in Milan and she was blown away by the contemporary dance we saw. Of course she knows what it's all about, because of the stuff we do at school, but she'd really like to try it for herself. With you. Just a few steps, a little routine, something like that. That was everything, wasn't it?' she asked, turning to Laila, who pushed her hands so deep into her pockets that it almost looked as though they might rip. Then she just nodded and looked down at the ground.

Lucas had an impenetrable expression on his face – it was a mixture of surprise, curiosity, doubt and delight. He cleared his throat, looked up, then simply said, 'Fine by me. We could meet at school, um, tomorrow morning? At eleven? I'll bring the music. Erm . . . Right then.' He slipped down from the bench and stood up. 'Got to go, I'm meeting . . . um, a friend. See you then,' he said, and loped away casually, his head held high, like an experienced athlete.

'I think he's really annoyed,' Laila said after a while, as she watched Lucas disappearing into the distance, 'but he didn't say so because of you. He didn't want to disappoint you.'

'I don't think so,' Zoe said carefully. 'One of the nice things about Lucas is his honesty. He'd never do something he didn't want to just to please someone else. And he really doesn't have much respect for me, you know. Sometimes he's almost rude.'

'Rude? I doubt that.' She rocked on her feet. 'Okay then, I'm going home. Thanks, Zoe. See you tomorrow. You'll come in as well, won't you? I don't think I'll be able to do it on my own.'

'What do you mean, you're going home?' said Zoe. 'No, no, no! Absolutely no chance. At the very least we'll have an ice cream together. No, not one of those nasty artificial things,' she added as Laila looked at the ice cream van by the park gates. 'A proper ice cream, a nice one, sitting down like two proper grown-up ladies. Okay?' She didn't give Laila any time to respond, but jumped down from the bench and, grabbing her arm, dragged her in the direction of the café. Laila stumbled, but regained her balance and laughed.

The ice cream really was good, Zoe thought to herself, and Laila had started to thaw a little too. She was soon telling Zoe all about when she was little and how she really wanted to be a ballerina even then. She said she'd decided when she was four and it was all she ever thought about after that. She got her parents to take her to ballets and she stayed wide awake all the way through, completely captivated. Zoe soon felt as though she'd heard Laila's entire life story.

The next day, at the Academy, Laila seemed like another person entirely. The confident girl Zoe had been talking to at the café had given way to a Laila who seemed shy and a little intimidated, which was strange, given that she was in her favourite place: the rehearsal room.
They'd gone to Zoe's favourite room up on the top floor and, as the morning was fresh and cool, they threw the windows open wide. Instead of her usual practice clothes, Laila was wearing a violet leotard – it was a present from her aunt, she'd told Zoe in the changing room. It seemed that everyone in the family only ever gave her dance-related things. Zoe was wearing a blue one that she'd picked out in the dance shop near the school in Milan. Lucas was wearing a white T-shirt and black leggings. They all had bare feet.

Lucas had chosen a rather strange piece of music: Ravel's *L'enfant et les sortilèges*. It was strange because it might have been easier to start with something with a strong rhythm, even if it was a bit boring. The atmosphere of the piece was charged with hidden meanings, and it really felt as though there were a child hidden in there somewhere, chanting spells, just as the title of the music said, and you had to listen to the spells and do what they said, because it was magic and you had no choice.

They'd agreed that Lucas would dance some steps and the two of them would follow him, although Zoe was really just there for moral support. Lucas ran through the moves by himself, so they'd get the idea. He danced along the diagonal, performing a simple sequence, but it was very free and loose – danced by Lucas, even the simplest of steps looked amazing. He repeated it, with Zoe copying his movements. Then it was Laila's turn to join in.

For a while, they didn't look at each other and just concentrated on their own moves. Then, when the dance became more familiar and the steps felt natural, it seemed right to start watching each other. Zoe stopped after a while and leaned against the barre, watching the other two, and she could see how Laila's slight reserve, which was all part of her classical training, had disappeared. She relaxed, her body became looser and she was no longer dancing a series of steps, but one single, flowing dance. Lucas stopped dancing too. He walked over to the piano and stood there watching Laila, who continued alone, sure of herself now. The music soon ended, but Laila still carried on dancing for a while before gently coming to a stop. She looked at them as though she was waking up from a dream and said, 'Has it finished?'

They both laughed and she joined in the laughter, because she knew they weren't teasing her, just being friendly. 'Shall we start again?' Laila suggested.

'Don't you want to rest?' Lucas asked her.

'No, definitely not,' Laila said, so the music started again and so did they. This time, Lucas made the sequence more complicated but Laila had no problem at all getting the hang of it and repeating it.

At that point, Zoe felt that her task was over. She slipped away as quietly as possible and stood outside in the upstairs corridor, which was flooded with the bright and beautiful light of the summer morning.

She leaned on the window ledge and looked out over all the old roofs of the city and the skyline of domes and towers. Then she heard someone approaching, so she turned to look. It was Madame Olenska.

'Oh, I'm sorry, Madame.' Zoe stood up straight and stepped back from the window. Pupils weren't allowed to walk around the school in their dance clothes if they weren't on their way to or from a lesson.

'No need to apologise, Zoe. You're fine as you are. It's not term time now, so the rules don't apply. Can I keep you company for a while?' She leaned her elbows on the ledge, silently giving Zoe permission to do the same. She was dressed very smartly, in a sheer blouse with flowing sleeves and a dark green bow at the neck. Together, in silence, they looked out at the city. Then

Madame, looking straight ahead, said, 'You know, I'm very pleased with you, Zoe, with the way you treated Laila during the summer course. Gimenez told me that without you Laila would have been . . . well, lost. She's a girl who needs to open up more. She's too solitary, too closed off. Yes, I know what you're thinking. She's never exactly been the easiest of people to deal with, to say the least. I know she's never had a proper friend at school, but that's why I'm so pleased with you. You managed to overlook quite a few years of unfriendliness. It's not something everyone could do.'

'We're not really friends,' Zoe said slowly, because she didn't want to receive Madame Olenska's praise for something that wasn't true.

'I know what you're saying,' Madame Olenska replied, 'and it's not something that'll happen in a second, and it's not even necessary. I would never ask you to make friends with her. These things happen by themselves if they're going to. The important thing is that Laila's softened a little. She's realised that other people don't always have to be rivals. Sometimes they can actually even help you, the way Lucas is helping her now.'

As always, Zoe was amazed at the way Madame Olenska knew everything and understood everything, even things she didn't appear to have seen or heard herself. It was as though everything in the school – the walls, the mirrors, the curtains, the barre – whispered what they saw to her.

'Are you going on holiday?' Zoe asked, trying to relieve the slight tension that their serious conversation had created.

'Oh, yes. I'm off on Sunday. I'm going to the Côte d'Azur, to stay at an old friend's villa. Complete isolation. When I'm at his place, I lose any desire for contact with the outside world. He always has quite a few guests – interesting people, but no one ever imposes themselves on anyone else. It's the ideal holiday.'

Zoe had a fleeting vision of her headmistress wearing a seaside version of her turbans, in pretty floral patterns instead of her normal dark colours, which were so wintry, so Russian, and a collection of long, soft kaftans. She could see her walking barefoot beside a swimming pool, reading in the shade on a patio, laughing as she spoke Russian with her old friend, who was probably a count with a big white beard and a mysterious past.

'Goodbye then, Zoe,' Madame said, waking Zoe from her brief daydream. 'See you in September. Have fun – you deserve it. And tell the other two,' she said, nodding in the direction of the rehearsal room, 'that I'd like to say goodbye to them as well. Please ask them to come to my office when they've finished.'

And so Madame left and Zoe went back to contemplating the city from on high. They really must be growing up if Madame took them so seriously that she actually wanted to say goodbye to them individually. It was as though they were no longer just students – the indistinct, chattering mass that usually swarmed through the corridors – but individuals. One of the good things about growing up, she thought, was that other people, adults, started to see you as you really were. As yourself.

CHAPTER TEN

A Rainy Day

'What shall we do?' asked Alice.

It was two weeks later and Zoe was on holiday with Alice. Zoe stretched out lazily on the top bunk of Alice's bed and watched the rain running down the slanting roof window. 'Well, I suggest we do nothing,' she said.

'That's exactly what I had in mind. Ed and Luke were going to try to make us play Risk with them.'

'No chance. I always lose. I don't intend to be humiliated again by your brothers and their complicated strategies. Anyway, it's the first rainy day.

Let's just enjoy doing nothing.'

'You're right. Ten days of constant sunshine. It was starting to feel weird.'

'It felt like we were in Spain or something,' agreed Zoe.

'Exactly.'

The mountain holiday with her family, and Alice and her family, who they had met on a previous trip, had been wonderful so far: ten days of sunshine and increasingly challenging walks. They'd climbed uphill for hours and hours, with rucksacks on their backs, and a feeling of euphoria hit them when they got to the top. They felt as though they were on top of the world and, in a way, they were. They could finally rest for a while and have a chat, because they couldn't talk too much when they were walking or they'd break their rhythm. The two families knew each other quite well by now and they usually went off on their hikes together. Even Sara, who could sometimes be a bit of a moody teenager, seemed quite happy to join in with the daily schedule.

'How come she never makes friends with anyone?' Alice had asked Zoe the day before, as she looked at Sara walking a few steps ahead of them. Her long blond hair was in a sensible plait and her legs looked really tanned against the white of her socks, which were folded down over her hiking boots. She somehow managed to look quite elegant even in her big boots, which made most people look as if they had clumsy animal hooves.

'Oh, I don't know,' Zoe had said. Then, just guessing, she'd added, 'She's had a few problems with her schoolwork this year. She's got a lot of catching up to do over the holidays. I think her mind's been full of her boyfriend, to be honest.'

'Whereas your mind, of course, is completely empty. You know why? You've got too many boys to choose from! So you can afford not to choose at all.'

Zoe's only response had been to stick her tongue out at Alice, who laughed, and the discussion was over, partly because they were just starting to climb a really daunting hill.

Thinking about it now, watching the rain, Zoe told herself that Alice was wrong, because she really couldn't see herself as a fair maiden with a whole line of potential suitors – well, only two actually.

Zoe thought that Sara must have been suffering a bit of heartache though, because Stephen, Sara's best friend and current boyfriend, was doing a language course abroad somewhere. He was going horse-riding and having loads of fun – too much fun for her liking, she'd said. She admitted she was actually jealous. So she took her mobile everywhere with her, even though it wasn't usually possible to get a signal, so it was pretty useless. To be honest, it was really annoying whenever she received a text message. Hearing that *beep beep* in the middle of a wood wasn't at all right, but there was no persuading her to leave it behind. The idea of being like Sara, depending on a *beep beep* to put a huge smile on your face when it arrived, and spoil your whole day if it didn't, made Zoe feel rather ill.

'Maybe you're just reverting to childhood,' Alice remarked when Zoe voiced her thoughts. 'You've gone back to being a little girl. Perhaps it's a touch of Peter Pan syndrome – in which case, it's pretty serious.'

'Don't be silly,' said Zoe.

'Oh, I was just joking,' replied Alice. 'It's so easy to pull your leg. Sometimes, the way you react, you're just like a little girl, which does give more support for my theory! I want to believe you, Zoe, but how can you be so sure that you're not suffering from Peter Pan syndrome?'

'Because I know I want to grow up. And I can prove it. Firstly, it's been at least six months since I last bought myself a cuddly toy,' Zoe said.

'I thought Maria was the big toy collector in your family, not you,' Alice pointed out. 'But go on.'

'Secondly, I didn't bring a copy of *Bambi* on holiday with me like I used to.'

'Of course you didn't. Because you knew there wasn't a DVD player here. Nope, still not good enough. But please continue.'

'Thirdly, I like it when Roberto and André text me or phone me.'

'Yes, of course you do. Go on.'

'Fourth . . . Er, fourthly . . .'

'You can't think of anything, can you?' teased Alice.

Zoe racked her brains. Then she laughed at herself.
'What is it I'm supposed to be proving to you?'

'To me? Nothing. As if! I've decided I'm not leaving
home until I'm at least twenty-five. It's far too nice at
home, with Mum and Dad looking after me. Maybe I'm
going on about Peter Pan because I'm the one who
doesn't want to grow up. It must be said that you're
rather strange though; you've had an experience that
anyone would envy – I mean, going away by yourself to
do a serious dance course – but you've hardly said a word
about it. You've got this gorgeous boy, who also happens
to be French, who's thinking about you from faraway,
and you're not even that bothered.'

'Just imagine how boring it would be if all I did was
tell you what I'd done on the summer course. Or if I
just talked about André. It'd drive you crazy.'

'That *is* true. Then again, how many times a day do
I mention my boyfriend?'

Zoe pretended to think about it, then said, 'No more
than twenty. I'd say it's just about bearable. But I warn
you, make it twenty-one and I'll start screaming.'

'There you go. You see? All it means is that I'm a
normal girl of my age. You, on the other hand, are
exceptional.'

'Oh, don't be silly.'

'No, you're the silly one. My brothers would do anything for you. And they don't treat you the way they treat me.'

'Of course not – you're their sister. They have to put up with you all year round, but I'm something new.'

'No. It's more than that. You're . . . It's strange, Zoe, but I'm being serious now, so listen to me and don't laugh. You're not perfect. If you were perfect, you'd be unbearable, like that Laila girl in your class. Just as well she's showing signs of improvement. Whereas you, you seem normal, but you're not. You really are special. And I'm saying that without any envy at all, honestly. You manage to be special without becoming unpleasant. You do the things you do very well, but you don't have to make sure that everyone else knows all about it. You're a wonderful ballerina . . . No, don't pull that face, I know it's true, but you don't make a big deal of it. That's just the way it is. You're really pretty, but you don't keep flicking your hair the way your sister does, and all those other girls who know just how pretty they are. And that's basically why everyone adores you. Boys *and* girls. Because you're special.'

Then she fell silent. It could have been embarrassing if the silence had gone on too long. Alice was so nice, though, that she made sure that didn't happen. So, after having showered Zoe with compliments, she concluded, 'And as if that weren't enough, you can eat whatever you want and you don't put on an ounce. Anyway, look at the time, Skinny Minnie. I think it's snack o'clock. Can you smell that delicious smell?'

'That must be your mum's apple pie,' Zoe said, sniffing the air.

'Exactly. So let's go down and demolish it. I think I've put on weight just from the smell, but I don't care. Come on!'

And a few short seconds later they'd slipped off the bed and were down the stairs and into the kitchen, where indeed the miraculous pie was just coming out of the oven.

'You don't want to eat it until it's cool,' Alice's mum said. She looked at their faces and added, 'Oh, do what you like. Today's one of those days, isn't it? What can you do except eat and sleep? I'll go and light the fire. That'll be nice and cosy.'

Alice's brothers, drawn by the irresistible aroma, came to join them in the kitchen. With four of them there, the pie wouldn't take long to finish. Alice hissed threateningly at her brothers. 'Leave some for Mum and Dad, you piggies,' and by some miracle, a quarter of the pie was left.

'So how about that game of Risk?' Luke suggested, licking crumbs off his top lip.

'Oh, you two can play. I hate losing,' Zoe said.

'Okay then. Let's play "If you were . . ." You don't have to think too hard about that,' Ed said. 'I'll start. If you were a flower, you would be a cornflower. If you were a colour, you'd be . . . blue. If you were a book, you'd be an adventure story with a happy ending. If you were a fruit, you'd be a peach.'

'I know! I know!' Luke said, bouncing on his chair. 'It's Zoe.'

'Why couldn't it be your sister?' Zoe asked. 'They're all things that could be about her too.'

'Oh, no,' Luke said, very seriously. 'Alice is red, she's a daisy, she's a science-fiction book, and an apple. And that's a fact.'

They all laughed together, and that's how Alice's mum found them.

'Aw, you're all so sweet when you're laughing like that. So maybe I'll forgive you for having polished off my pie so quickly that I bet you didn't even taste it properly. I was thinking I might make some jam, given the weather. Who wants to help me?'

Before long, the kitchen had turned into the assembly line of a jam factory and it was filled with the scent of hot fruit and sugar, which blended with the lingering aroma of the tart, and was even more delicious, if that was possible.

Zoe had never made jam before, but she certainly ate enough of it, and she watched the process with great interest. She just did the simplest jobs, such as washing and peeling the plums and spreading them out on the cloth, so that Alice's mum could pick them up, weigh them, then cook them with the right amount of sugar.

'I thought it was going to take ages,' she said when the jars were sealed and lined up on the shelf with their glowing contents.

'Well, it is almost time for dinner,' Alice's mum said. 'Your mum and dad suggested that we should all have a pizza tonight, over at your place. Your dad and Sara are going to fetch them. We just have to make sure we're there in quarter of an hour. And we're all going to play charades afterwards.'

'Hey, do you think adults have Peter Pan syndrome too?' Zoe said to Alice as they were going upstairs to fetch their sweatshirts. 'Pizza, charades . . .'

'Why, don't you want to play? It's fun once a year.'

'I wonder what Sara's going to think of it.'

Surprisingly, Sara was one of the ones who had most fun. For once she appeared to have left her mobile phone somewhere – she didn't look at it once that evening. Instead, she took care of the younger ones, who were eating at a separate table by the window, and she was really nice to everyone and didn't do her usual sulky teenager routine. She didn't play with her hair the way she usually did and she didn't look daggers at Zoe and Alice the way she usually did and . . . she ate a pizza and a half all by herself, without paying any attention to the calories.

'I think all that rain must have made her brain all soggy – she's not thinking normally,' Zoe whispered in Alice's ear.

'Don't be such a meanie,' Alice hissed back to her. 'It's nice spending some time with your family every now and then. She knows that.'

Zoe looked at the faces around the big table, at her friends and her sisters and the four grown-ups, and listened as the adults talked about plans for a trip if the weather was good the next day. Everyone looked so happy and relaxed. Zoe realised that Alice was right. She loved spending time with her family – and with Alice's family too. The two families shared an unusual kind of friendship. They could be apart for a long time, but then settle into a familiar routine the moment they were back together again. Zoe thought how lucky they were to know each other.

'Do you know something?' Zoe said to Alice. 'I like having a family this big. I mean with you and your lot. What do they call it? An extended family, that's it.'

'Me too,' Alice mumbled, catching a falling chunk of tomato in mid-air. 'Me too. Who cares if it's raining tomorrow? We'll find something to do. All of us together.'

'Yes, together,' Zoe echoed.

CHAPTER ELEVEN

Summer's Almost Over

It's strange how you can have such different kinds of holiday, Zoe thought. The summer course in Milan had been a holiday, the kind that involved going to a new place and seeing all kinds of new things, which stimulated your curiosity and your mind. Going away on the hiking trip had been a holiday too. It was a familiar place, but Zoe never got tired of its beauty, and it was lovely to spend time with people she knew, precisely because she knew them so well. In fact, she never got tired of seeing the people she genuinely liked.

The way the calendar fell meant that school was

starting a week later than usual this year, so Zoe's mum and dad had decided that there was time to squeeze in a few more days away. They were all staying with Zoe's gran at a little hotel in a seaside village, which was really quiet now that the main summer holiday was over. They were enjoying the lovely weather – the days were still warm even though the evenings were already cooler. There wasn't much of the summer left, so every moment felt special.

The hotel was right on the seafront, built on the cliffs on a small headland. Looking out of the window of the room she was sharing with her sisters, Zoe felt like she was on a sailing ship anchored in the port, ready to set sail when the captain said it was time. The waves crashing against the rocks was an unusual background sound, but she soon got used to it. Maria, with all the contrariness of a seven-year-old, declared that she couldn't sleep because of the noise of the sea, but she dropped off the moment her head touched the pillow.

Sara had been in a gloomy mood for three days, until she'd met a group of local teenagers who got together every evening in the park and since then she'd cheered up no end. During the daytime, her new friends almost all had jobs in local businesses, lending a hand in ice cream parlours, shops and restaurants, and Sara took advantage of the free time to go sunbathing. She disappeared around five o'clock and an hour later Zoe would see her crossing the hotel lobby as she headed for her usual appointment, perfectly made up, beautifully dressed, and surrounded by a cloud of verbena. All three sisters used the same verbena-scented shower gel. Sara complained about that a bit, because she'd been the one to discover it, but Zoe really liked the smell. It was a little bit like lemon and a little bit like grass, and seemed almost to change according to your mood.

Zoe spent her time having fun with her gran, who wasn't keen on the beach or the swimming pool. In the mornings, they walked along the seafront, picked a bench, sat down and closed their eyes in the sun like two cats, talking a bit, then just sitting in silence. Then they got up and went to the shops to look for clothes for the coming autumn. Gran had bought Zoe a lacy mauve cardigan. When she first saw it, Zoe thought it was a very granny kind of colour, except for the fact that her own gran preferred bright colours – shocking pink, apple green, electric blue – so it seemed strange that she'd choose mauve for her granddaughter. 'Do you think I seem like a mauve kind of person, Gran?' she asked her after they'd bought the cardigan.

'Yes, absolutely,' her gran said. 'And why not powder pink? And dusty blue too? You should experiment. Everything in your life is so vague and undecided at your age – no offence, of course.'

'None taken. I told you I liked it. And you could be right about my life . . .'

'Of course I'm right,' her gran said. 'There's nothing bad about being at an age when things are still undecided. In fact, I think it's a wonderful privilege, and a right too. You don't always have to know exactly what it is that you want. The world isn't completely black and white. There are all sorts of subtle shades in between, thank goodness.'

'Yes, but you're not so keen on the subtle shades, are you?' Zoe said, looking pointedly at her gran's cardigan with its pattern of red, black and violet shapes.

'It's just that I don't like dressing the way people expect someone of my age to dress, that's all,' her gran explained. 'I may be old but I don't feel at all fragile and floral. Not that I think you're the floral type, or anything. I've never thought that. But maybe you still need to decide what colour you are.'

'When we were on holiday, Ed said that if I were a colour, I'd be blue.'

'Yes, that's quite possible,' her gran said after a moment's thought. 'Or maybe violet, which isn't so far from blue. You just have to add a little red.'

'If I were a cake, I'd like to be a chocolate éclair,' Zoe said, suddenly changing the subject, as they walked past the best baker's in town.

'You'd like to *be* a chocolate éclair or you'd like to *have* one?' her gran asked with a smile. Without hesitating, she went into the shop and asked for two chocolate éclairs to eat straightaway.

They left the shop and for a while they didn't look in shop windows or talk. They just immersed themselves in the wonderful flavour of chocolate and cream melting on their tongues.

'It's so good to give in to temptation every now and then,' Zoe's gran said when she'd finished her éclair. 'Do you know what I mean? Anyway, that's my walk done for today. I'm going back to the hotel to pick a nice spot on the terrace and carry on reading my thriller.'

The sun was so hot that it felt like the height of summer, and Zoe was quite happy to leave her gran to her exciting book and go to the hotel swimming pool. Very few of the sun loungers were occupied, and her favourite one, with a view of the sea, was free. Mum, Dad and the others weren't there; they preferred the beach, but she liked the beach better towards the evening, when it was a bit emptier and you felt as though you had the sky and sea all to yourself. Right now, she wanted to rest her gaze on the smooth and impossibly blue surface of the swimming pool, with its tiny ripples blown by the breeze.

Almost directly opposite her sat a couple who were obviously foreigners and seemed very much in love. They both had very blond, almost white hair and pale skin and they held hands wherever they went, looking into each other's eyes, talking away and laughing. She'd never seen one of them without the other. She thought they were so romantic, sweet without being soppy: they were simply very happy.

I'm happy too, Zoe thought, as she took her eyes off the couple. She was wearing sunglasses so they couldn't see she was looking, but it still felt wrong to stare. Instead, she looked out at the sea, which was divided into vertical strips by the white rails around the terrace. *I've had such a wonderful summer,* she thought. *It's been nice in so many different ways. But now it's almost time to start school again and I'm looking forward to it. I've had so many different experiences with friends this summer. And everything's turned out pretty well – with Laila, Leda, Alice, Lucas and Roberto... And with André too.*

She was sure she'd start really looking forward to things soon, when it was time to pack her suitcases one last time and put them down on the floor of the hotel bedroom.

Leda had phoned her five times in five days and had swamped her with text messages that were so silly they didn't require a response: she was already back home, she was bored, she had so many things to tell Zoe and she had so many things to ask her. Laila had phoned her too, but only once: she said she was happy that school was starting again soon, and that she'd made some new friends on holiday. Zoe hadn't heard anything from Roberto and André in the last few days, but it didn't bother her.

The sun was warming her skin and she slowly did an exercise in concentration, thinking about the muscles beneath her skin and feeling them tensing at her command and answering her call. Well, she could feel all of the big important ones, but there were others that were beyond her control; she'd have to wake them up again slowly and calmly. The patient exercise of rediscovery and mastery at the barre would do the trick.

The maybe husband-and-wife, maybe girlfriend-and-boyfriend got up, hands laced together, walked around the swimming pool and smiled at her as they passed. As they walked away, she heard the woman whisper to the man, 'Look, it's the ballerina!' Could they tell just by looking at her? Or had they been watching her the way she'd watched them and worked it out by the way she moved? Zoe knew very well that anyone who'd studied ballet had a very distinctive walk, and she was pleased that two strangers might have seen that in her.

She was on her own. And now, without feeling at all silly or theatrical, but just because she was in the mood, she stood up, using the rail as a barre and slowly, in her bare feet, started to do a few warm-up exercises. In the sun, in the fresh air, with the sky and the sea meeting felt so different. She had a sensation of of pure freedom. Her leg was extended in a , *grand battement* when Maria, dressed in her swimming costume, burst on to the terrace, from the steps leading down to the beach, shouting and squealing and followed by her dad, who caught hold of her and picked her up. The two of them stood still, in a hug, watching Zoe, suspended in the moment. Then Zoe lowered her leg and they came forward. Maria slipped out of her dad's hug, started running again and flew straight to Zoe and hugged her around the waist. 'Was I dreaming that you were practising ballet?' she said, looking up at Zoe, with a happy grin and messy hair.

'Maybe,' Zoe answered. She let go of the barre – no, the railing – and responded to Maria's hug, burying her face in her little sister's hair, which smelled of salt and verbena.

'You're always on your own. Are you feeling a bit sad?' Maria whispered to her, as though she didn't want their dad to hear.

'No, not at all. I'm happy. Sometimes you can be happy even when you're on your own, you know.'

Maria pulled a funny face. That was something she didn't really understand. Then she slipped out of the hug, ran over to the swimming pool and did an almost perfect dive. She surfaced with a huge smile and said, 'See how good I am?' Zoe's dad walked over to Zoe and put his arm around her shoulders. They both nodded at Maria and grinned. She got out of the swimming pool and her dad took the towel from around his shoulders and held it out to her, wrapping her up in a towelly hug, and rubbing her little body to warm her up. Her hair was streaming down on to her shoulders and she was glowing with pleasure. You could see how happy she was, that she didn't want to be anywhere else in the world. Zoe smiled back at her, because she felt exactly the same way.

Their mum was next to arrive. She was wearing new sunglasses, which had big lenses and a thick dark green frame and gave her a mysterious and slightly distant air. With her reddish hair, they really suited her. Even though you couldn't see her eyes, her smile said it all. It said she was happy to see these three people she loved.

They were only missing Sara to make the moment perfect. It was anyone's guess where she was. Zoe suspected she'd stayed down on the beach a little longer and when she leant out over the railing, she spotted her down there, lying stretched out on her tummy, with her iPod headphones sticking in her ears, and a foot, just the one, moving to a rhythm that only she knew. She was there with them really, just a few metres away. So, the whole family was together. They really needed a camera, Zoe thought, but, as so often happens, it's not easy to capture perfection. The memory would have to be enough.

The moment passed. All it took was Maria starting to talk again, in her usual loud voice, 'I looked at the menu this morning, but I don't remember what there was. Did they have something with chips? I'd like something with chips. I don't know what though. Anyone remember what's on the menu? Ooh, I'm not even sure what I fancy.'

'With your appetite,' their dad said, 'I think you'll happily gobble down whatever they serve.'

'Well, I want to grow up as quickly as possible,' Maria said. 'I want to be at least as big as Zoe. Then I can go on the plane by myself and have boyfriends and buy the clothes I want and . . .'

Their gran came over from the quiet side of the terrace, with the white beach umbrellas and the wicker chairs. 'If you come for a walk with me today, Maria, you can pick out something to wear for yourself. Just one thing though,' she said.

'You spoil her too much,' their dad said. 'You'll turn her into a right little madam.'

'Oh, that's not fair,' their gran replied. 'I spoilt the other two just as much, and I don't think they're too terrible, are they?'

'Not at all,' their mum said, slipping off her glasses. Now Zoe could see her expression: it was so warm, calm and reassuring. 'I think they're turning out very well indeed.'

'Yes, I agree, but let's not be too generous with the compliments, eh? The slightest thing could be enough to turn them into scary monsters,' their dad joked. 'Come on, it's time to get ready for dinner. Who's going to wake up Sleeping Beauty?' He looked down at the beach.

'I'll go,' Zoe said, and she was already off down the steps. She ran down, taking them two by two, with little leaps. She still had bare feet. She'd left her flip-flops by the side of the pool and would have to remember to fetch them. Her feet sank into the sand, which was warm on the surface, but the chilly layer beneath almost made her shiver. One of the clearest memories she had of previous summers by the sea was the midday heat forcing her to jump from one circle of shade to another, performing a strange kind of ballet amongst the beach umbrellas.

She stood over Sara and made a shadow on her to get her attention. Sara didn't notice straightaway – maybe she thought it was just a cloud passing over the sun. She eventually turned over and, when she saw it was Zoe, she smiled. 'Ah, what a lovely sight,' she said. 'I was starting to get bored and my stomach's rumbling away to itself. If you're here, it must mean what I was hoping: it's nearly time to eat.'

'Absolutely,' Zoe said to her, smiling. 'You can really

work up an appetite, lying in the sun.'

'You'd be surprised. I think I'll have the fish. It's not too fattening and it's good for your brain. I need a little brain food or I'm not sure I'm going to be able to handle next year. At school, I mean,' she said, as if there were any need to explain. Then she suddenly changed the subject, as she often did. 'You know, it's been a while since we spent some time together. Maybe we could go down to the front together later, have a bit of a chat. If you feel like it, that is,' she added, hastily.

'Yeah, maybe,' Zoe said.

'And this evening we could go out for a drink, just the two of us. I'm actually a bit bored of the kids down the park. All they talk about is parties and shoes and clothes and the fabulous holidays they're going to have once the season's over here. Do you know what they do? They all close up the businesses for three months and head off to the Seychelles, or the Maldives or Mexico. They get home-schooled and you know what else? They say it's a real drag, because there's nothing to do when they get there – no discos, no nightclubs. The idiots! I think that doing absolutely nothing on an exotic island would be wonderful. Sure, you've got to know how to enjoy yourself. They're just not capable. I, on the other hand, am sure that I'd be really good at it. I bet you would too.'

'Yes, I think I would,' Zoe said. 'You could always

take a suitcase full of books.'

'Or you could paint.'

'Or knit.'

'Or do crosswords.'

'Or just lie there thinking. Or not even doing that much. Just watching the clouds float by. The skies in those kinds of places are always full of beautiful clouds, aren't they?'

'Do you remember when we were little and we used to play at spotting animal shapes in the clouds?'

'Of course I do,' Zoe said. 'You always said you could see a man on a horse.'

'And you always saw an elephant. Then one day you said you saw a ballerina, and the next day too, then you started drawing ballet shoes and tutus and I knew that we'd lost you.'

Zoe laughed. 'That's not true. It was Leda who always used to draw things to do with dancing.'

'Hmm, maybe. But you know what little kids are like. One of them does something and the other has to copy it.'

'But I chose to dance myself.'

'No, you didn't. You were too little. It was Mum and Dad who chose ballet for you. The same way they tried horse-riding with me. But horses are too big and scary for my liking. I prefer volleyball.'

'But I kept it up, didn't I?'

'Exactly. For a while I wondered whether it was just because you didn't have much imagination or because Leda did it and the two of you were inseparable, or you just didn't want to let Mum down, or maybe you weren't interested in anything else.'

'And?'

'And nothing. I stopped wondering about it. They were all just silly doubts. You were so happy. You're still so happy.'

'Can you tell?'

'Of course. You can see that you're doing just fine. Maybe you'll have problems one day, I don't know. Maybe you won't. But you know, the other evening you were all out for a walk after your ice cream, and I was with that lot from the park . . . Well, I saw you and I pointed you out and said, "See her? That's my sister. She's a ballerina" and one of them said, "Oh, yes. You can tell, she looks really graceful." He was pretty cute, by the way. Now that I'm thinking about it, you really should come out with me this evening. I could introduce you to him. How about it?'

'But weren't we going to . . .'

'Ah, that's right. Silly me. I'd already suggested something for tonight. A drink. Together. The two of us. On our own. Two good little sisters who have so many stories to tell each other. For example, that André? You've hardly said a word about him, but he looks such a sweetheart in the group photo you showed me. So, is he *your* sweetheart?'

'I don't know,' Zoe said. It was an honest answer.

'Fine, I get it. I'm being nosy. End of subject. Hey, will you teach me to walk the way you do, like a ballerina? How about you walk ahead and I'll copy you?'

So that's how they walked back to the hotel, Zoe five steps ahead, Sara following, carefully putting one foot in front of the other, shoulders down, head high, neck straight.

'Ooh, it's such hard work,' Sara said when they finally got there, collapsing against the railing. 'I give up. Let's forget about it. It really is true that ballerinas are born, not made.'

They walked into the hotel lobby, arm in arm, one ballerina and one non-ballerina, simply two sisters together.

Ballet Academy

BEATRICE MASINI

Have you read them all?

Book 1
Dance Steps

Another term at Ballet Academy brings even tougher challenges for Zoe and her friends. Leda is growing too tall and Laila is making everyone miserable. And then there's the end of term show to put on . . .

Book 2
A Question of Character

As Zoe begins character dance classes, life seems to become more eventful – Leda is turning frosty, but Roberto seems friendlier than ever!

Book 3
Friends Old and New

With Madame Olenska away, a new teacher brings a new style of teaching to the Academy – how will everyone react? Lucas is also offered the chance of a lifetime and the reason for Alissa's absence is discovered.

Ballet Academy

BEATRICE MASINI

Book 5
Dancing in Milan

Zoe's over the moon – she's been chosen to take part in a dance course in Italy! There's only one problem – Laila is going too and when they are together, sparks usually fly . . .

It will also give Zoe a chance to meet Roberto's family who live in Milan, and spend some time with him, but she and Roberto haven't been getting on very well lately so will this be a good or bad thing?

Coming Soon:
Book 6
A Tutu Too Many

A new student, Donna, joins the Ballet Academy, and is staying with Zoe and her family. It's not long before Zoe is feeling stifled, feeling that she has someone watching her all the time and has to involve Donna in everything she does.

As if that weren't enough, Madame Olenska is growing unhappy with the whole class, sparking off all kinds of doubts for the young ballerinas . . .

Ballet Academy

BEATRICE MASINI

The World of Ballet

Step into the wonderful world of ballet!
This beautifully illustrated book is filled with
everything you love about ballet – all the steps and
jumps, the stunning costumes, the best-loved ballets
and your favourite ballet stars are revealed by
Zoe and her Ballet Academy friends.

Discover behind-the-scenes secrets and find out
everything you ever wanted to know about the elegant,
graceful, amazing world of ballet!

Ballet Academy

Join in at:

www.balletacademy.co.uk

Discover more about:
★ the books
★ the dancing
★ the Academy
★ and lots more!

If you've enjoyed Ballet Academy,
you'll love these other titles from Piccadilly Press!

Sand Dancers

Let the Dance Begin

Lynda Waterhouse

All the Sand Dancers are very excited –
the Sandringham Dance School is going to reopen!
Cassie is desperate to win a place. Not only
does she love dancing, but she is sure that the school
holds the answers to her mother's disappearance.
Cassie's mother, the prima donna dancer, vanished
on the night of the Great Sandstorm seven years earlier.
No one seems to know what happened to her and the
dance school has been closed ever since – until now!

As Cassie investigates, she uncovers a story of jealousy,
betrayal, love, and friendship . . .

Girl Writer

Castles
and
Catastrophes

Ros Asquith

Cordelia Arbuthnott wants to write books. Not the sort that her aunt, the bestselling children's author Laura Hunt writes, but literary masterpieces.

So when she finds out that her dreaded new school Falmer North is having a writing competition, she's delighted. She just knows her medieval love story, *The Lady of the Rings*, will win the romance category.

But writing a masterpiece is trickier than she expected. What with wanting to make a good impression at Falmer North, sorting out her best friend Callum's home problems, and coping with her eccentric family, real life just keeps getting in the way.

Featuring fantastic top tips on getting your story right.

SHERIDAN WINN

THE
Sprite
Sisters

THE CIRCLE OF POWER

'I've got a magic trick!'
said Ariel. 'Watch!'
She pointed her finger at Flame's purple bra.
It lifted off the chair and hovered in the air.
Marina and Ash laughed.

Each of the Sprite Sisters, aged between nine and thirteen, has a magical power related to one of the four elements – Earth, Water, Fire or Air. When Ariel discovers her power on her ninth birthday, their circle is complete. The girls' magic must be kept secret, and used only for good; if not, the consequences could be dire.

The Sprites' big house in the country is full of laughter and sunshine, but a shadow is falling. Everything the Sprite Sisters hold dear will soon be shattered by the arrival of someone who is intent on destroying their power . . .